Gary GORTON

W9-ADC-598

THE ROAD TO THE CITY

Books by Natalia Ginzburg

All Our Yesterdays

Family Sayings

The Little Virtues

The City and the House

The Manzoni Family

Valentino and Sagittarius

*Family: Family and Borghesia,
   Two Novellas*

Voices in the Evening

The Road to the City

NATALIA
GINZBURG

THE ROAD
TO THE CITY
TWO NOVELLAS

Translated from the Italian
by Frances Frenaye

ARCADE PUBLISHING • NEW YORK
Little, Brown and Company

First U.S. Edition 1990

"The Road to the City" was originally published in Italian under the title *La strada che va in città*.
"The Dry Heart" was originally published in Italian under the title *È stato così*.

The characters and events in this book are fictitious. Any similarity to real persons, living or dead, is coincidental and not intended by the author.

Library of Congress Cataloging-in-Publication Data
Ginzburg, Natalia.
    [Strada che va in città. English]
    The road to the city ; and, The dry heart : two novellas / Natalia Ginzburg ; translated from the Italian by Frances Frenaye.
        p.   cm.
    Translation of: La strada che va in città and È stato così.
    ISBN 1-55970-052-1
    1. Ginzburg, Natalia — Translations, English. I. Ginzburg, Natalia. È stato così. 1990. II. Title. III. Title: Dry heart.
PQ4817.I5A6   1990
853'.912 — dc20   89-38521
                                                                          CIP

Published in the United States by Arcade Publishing, Inc., New York, a Little, Brown company

10 9 8 7 6 5 4 3 2 1

BP

PRINTED IN THE UNITED STATES OF AMERICA

TO LEONE

CONTENTS

The Road to the City   9

The Dry Heart   69

The labour of the foolish wearieth every one of them, because he knoweth not how to go to the city.

ECCLESIASTES X. 15

NINI was the son of one of my father's cousins and he had been with us ever since he was a little boy. After the death of his parents he went first to live with his grandfather, but the old man used to beat him with a broomstick and he was always running away to our house. Finally his grandfather died, too, and he was told he could stay with us always.

There were five of us, not counting Nini. The oldest was my sister, Azalea, who had married and gone to live in the city. I came next, and then my three brothers, Giovanni, Gabriele, and Vittorio. They say that big families are happy, but I could never see anything particularly happy about ours. Azalea had married and gone away when she was seventeen, and my one ambition was to do likewise. I was seventeen now myself, but I didn't have any offers. Giovanni and Nini were equally restless; in fact, the two smaller boys were the only ones content to stay where they were.

Our house was red with a pergola in front of it, and we hung our clothes on the banisters because we didn't have enough cupboards. 'Shoo, shoo!' my mother would say as she chased the hens out of the kitchen. 'Shoo, shoo!' All day long the gramophone played the same record over and over again:

> 'Velvety hands, your sweet perfu-u-me
> Seems to pervade this cosy roo-o-m . . .'

The cadence of this song enchanted us all and we sang it from the time we got up to the time we went to bed. Giovanni and Nini slept in the room next to mine and woke me up every morning with three knocks on the wall. I would get dressed in a hurry and we would all three set out for the city, which was an hour's walk away. When we got there we lost no time in separating, as if we were total strangers. I usually went to see a friend and strolled with her under the arcades. Sometimes I ran into Azalea with a red nose under her veil, but she refused to speak to me because I hadn't a hat.

Later in the morning I would eat bread and oranges down by the river or else go to see Azalea. Usually I found her in bed, smoking or reading a novel or having a jealous quarrel with her lover over the telephone, quite heedless of the presence of the children around her. Then her husband would come in for lunch and she would quarrel with him too. Her husband was an oldish man with eyeglasses and a beard. He seldom paid any attention to what she said but read his newspaper, sighing, scratching his head, and exclaiming to himself every now and then: 'God help us!' Then Ottavia, the fourteen-year-old servant girl, wearing her black hair in an untidy braid and carrying the baby in her arms, would announce from the door: 'Lunch is ready!' Azalea would pull on her stockings, yawn, and look down at her legs, and then we would all sit down at the table. Whenever the telephone rang Azalea blushed and twisted her napkin in her hands, while Ottavia answered from the next room: 'She's busy just now; she'll call you later.'

After lunch her husband always went out again and Azalea went back to bed, where she almost immediately fell asleep, with a calm and affectionate expression on her relaxed face. The telephone could ring, doors slam, and the children shout, but Azalea only breathed deeply and went on sleeping. While Ottavia cleared the table she used to ask me in a frightened manner what would happen if 'the master' were to find out. Then she would add in a low voice, with a bitter smile, that 'the master' had someone else too. At this point I would leave. I used to wait on a park bench for evening to fall, while my friend and I listened to the music coming from an outdoor café and looked at the dresses on the women passing by. Sometimes I would see Nini and Giovanni go by, but we never spoke. I was sure to meet them later on the dusty road outside the city, while the city lights went on behind us and the café orchestra struck up more gaily than before. We walked silently along the country road, between the river and the trees, until we reached home.

I hated our house. I hated my mother and the bitter sorrel soup that she set before us every evening. If I had met her in the city I should have been ashamed. But she had not gone to the city for years, and now, with her unkempt grey hair and missing front teeth, she seemed for all the world a peasant. 'You look like a witch, Mother,' Azalea would say when she came to the house. 'Why don't you get some false teeth?' Then she would lie down on the red couch in the dining-room, kick off her shoes, and say: 'Give me a cup of coffee.' After she had drunk down the coffee which my mother brought her she would take a nap and then go away. My mother always said that children were serpents' teeth and that no one had any business bringing them into the world. Indeed she spent all her days cursing her children, one by one.

When my mother was young a justice of the peace had fallen in love with her and carried her off to Milan. My mother was always telling this story, but she claimed that the justice of the peace was a figment of gossip and that she had gone away because she was tired of her children. 'If only I'd never come back!' she used to say, spreading her fingers over her face to wipe away her tears. My mother talked all the time, but I never answered. Only Nini answered her occasionally. He was very different from us in spite of the fact that we had grown up together. He had a pale face that never tanned in the sun and a lock of hair that tumbled over his forehead. He always had his pockets stuffed with books and newspapers, which he devoured unceasingly, even at mealtime. Just to be fresh, Giovanni would knock over whatever he was reading.

Nini would simply pick it up and go right on, running his fingers through his hair, while the gramophone blared:

'Velvety hands, your sweet perfume . . .'

My two younger brothers shouted and hit each other, and my mother pitched into me for not helping her with the dishes. My father would say that she should have brought me up better, and when she sobbed that everyone treated her like a dog he would take his hat down from the rack and go out. My father was an electrician, with photography as a side line, and he wanted to teach Giovanni to be an electrician too. But Giovanni was too lazy to answer any calls for a repair job. We never had enough money, and my father was always ill-humoured and tired. He would come in for a few minutes and then go away again, saying that the place was a madhouse. But he always said that it was his fault and my mother's, not ours, that we were so badly brought up. My father still looked young and my mother was very jealous. He always washed thoroughly before he went out and put brilliantine on his hair, and when I met him in the city I was not ashamed. Nini was a great one for washing, too, and he used to steal brilliantine from my father. But it failed to hold down the lock of hair that fell across his forehead.

One day Giovanni said to me:

'Nini drinks grape brandy.'

I stared at him in astonishment.

'Brandy? Does he drink it often?'

'Whenever he can. Just as often as he can lay his hands on it. He has a bottle of it hidden here at home. I found it and then he had to let me have some. It was good.'

'Nini drinks grape brandy!' I repeated unbelievingly to myself. I went to see Azalea and found her all alone in the kitchen, eating tomato salad with a vinegar dressing.

'Nini drinks grape brandy,' I said to her.

She shrugged her shoulders.

'Well, he's got to do something to keep from being bored, hasn't he?' she said.

'That's right. We're all bored. Why, I wonder?'

'Because life is boring,' she said, pushing away her plate. 'There's not much to do about it. Nothing gives one a kick for very long.'

'Why are we always so bored?' I said to Nini that evening on the way home.

'Who's bored, I'd like to know? Not I!' And he laughed and took my arm. 'Are you bored, then? Why, when everything's so beautiful?'

'What's beautiful?' I asked.

'Everything,' he said. 'I like the looks of everything I see. A while ago I enjoyed walking in the city, and now that we're walking in the country I enjoy that just as well.'

Giovanni was just a few steps ahead of us. He turned around and said: 'Nini's working in a factory now.'

'I'm learning to use a lathe,' said Nini, 'so I can make some money. It's too painful not having any. If I've just a little change jingling in my pocket I start feeling more cheerful. And it's a question of either stealing or earning it. That's something they've never explained properly at home. They're always bawling us out, but that's just their way of passing the time. No one's ever told us: "Shut up and get out!" And that's what we needed to hear.'

'If they'd said anything like that to me,' retorted Giovanni, 'I'd have put *them* out of the door in a hurry.'

On the road we met the doctor's son, who had been out hunting with his dog. He had shot seven or eight quail and gave two of them to me. He was a stoutish young man with a thick black moustache who was studying medicine at the university. He and Nini got into a discussion and later Giovanni said:

'Nini has ten times the brains of the doctor's son. Nini's no ordinary fellow, you know, even if he hasn't had much schooling.'

But I was all excited because Giulio had given me the quail and looked at me and said that one day we must go to the city together. Summer was coming on and I began to think of remodelling all my clothes. I told my mother that I had to have some light blue material, and she asked me where I thought she was going to get the money. Then I said that I had to have a pair of cork-soled shoes, too, and I threw in a curse at the mother that had borne her. She slapped me in the face, and I shut myself up in my room and cried all day long. Later I asked Azalea for the money. She sent me to a house at 20 Via Genova to ask if Alberto was there. I brought back the answer that he wasn't, and she gave me the money for pay. I stayed several days in my room sewing the dress and almost forgot about the city entirely. When the dress was finished I put it on and went out for a walk. The doctor's son caught up with me and bought some cakes and we ate them together in the woods. He asked me why I had been shut up in the house so long, and I told him that I didn't like to have other people pry into my affairs. He asked me not to be so hard on him and tried to kiss me, but I ran away.

I lay all morning on the balcony tanning my legs. I had the cork-soled shoes and the dress and a woven straw handbag that Azalea gave me for taking a letter to 20 Via Genova. My face and arms and legs soon took on a wonderful brown. The neighbours told my mother that Giulio, the doctor's son, was in love with me and that his parents were very upset about it. My mother turned agreeable all of a sudden and gave me an egg for breakfast every morning, because she said that I didn't seem up to par. The doctor's wife stood at her window with her maidservant beside her, and when I went by she closed it up as if she had seen a snake. Giulio half smiled and went right on walking beside me. I didn't listen to what he was saying, but I thought to myself that soon this stoutish young man with the black moustache and the riding boots, who whistled to his dog, would be engaged to me, and many a girl in the village would cry her eyes out.

2

'Azalea wants to see you,' Giovanni said to me one day after I hadn't been to the city for a long time. I put on my new dress and shoes and a pair of sunglasses. At Azalea's house everything was in disorder. The beds weren't made and Ottavia, with the children clinging to her skirts, was leaning up against the wall in tears.

'He's through with her,' she said. 'He's getting married.'

Azalea sat on the edge of the bed in her slip, with wide-open, flashing eyes. A pile of letters lay in her lap.

'He's getting married in September,' she said.

'We must hide all these things before the master comes back,' said Ottavia.

'We'll burn them, that's what we'll do,' said Azalea. 'I never want to see them again. I don't want to look at his stupid face either,' she added, tearing up the picture of a smiling Army officer. And she began to scream and sob, knocking her head against the foot of the bed.

'She's going to have convulsions,' said Ottavia. 'My mother used to have them too. We ought to put her in a cold bath.'

Azalea wouldn't let us do anything of the sort. She said that she wanted to be alone and that we should go and call her husband so that she could confess the whole story. We had quite a job talking her out of it. Finally we burned the letters in the kitchen stove, while Ottavia read passages out loud to me before she threw them into the flames, and the children chased pieces of charred paper all over the room. When Azalea's husband came home I told him that she was in bed with a fever and he went to get a doctor.

It was night when I reached home, and my father asked

me where I'd been. I told him that Azalea had sent for me, and Giovanni put in a word to say that it was true. My father said that for all he knew it might be so, but he had heard I was going around with the doctor's son, and if this was the case he'd smash my face for me. I said that I would do what I pleased, regardless, and then I lost my temper and threw my soup on the floor. I shut myself up in my room and cried for two or three hours until Giovanni called to me from next door to be quiet and let them sleep. I went on crying and finally Nini came to the door and said he'd give me some chocolates. I opened the door and Nini made me look at my swollen face in the mirror and gave me the promised chocolates, which he said he had got from his girl. I asked what his girl was like, and he said she had wings and a tail and wore a geranium in her hair. I said that I was engaged, too, to the doctor's son.

'Very good,' he said, but he grimaced and got up to go. I asked him where he kept his bottle of brandy, and he said that was none of a girl's business.

The next night Nini didn't come home, or the night after, either. We didn't see hide or hair of him for some time, and even my father, who rarely noticed anything, asked where he had gone. Giovanni said that he was all right but that for the time being he was staying away.

'Boys come home as long as it suits them,' said my father, 'and then when they find something better, it's good-bye. They're all alike, the lot of them.'

Giovanni told me that Nini was with his girl, a young widow called Antonietta. I went to the city for the express purpose of finding out if this was true. And there I came upon him sitting with Giovanni in the café, eating ice-cream. I sat down and had some ice-cream, too, and we stayed there a while listening to the music. When we left Nini paid the bill like a gentleman. I asked him if it was true about the widow and he said it was, and why didn't I come to the little apartment where he was living with her and her two children. Antonietta owned a stationery shop, he said, and did a fairly good business.

'So you're living off her, are you?' I said.

'What do you mean?' he answered. 'I'm earning good pay.' And he said he was getting ahead in the factory and hoped soon to send some money back home.

The next time I was in the woods, smoking a cigarette with Giulio, I told him about Nini and how I had gone to see him.

'You shouldn't do a thing like that,' he said.

'Why?'

'There are things you're too much of a child to understand.'

I told him that I wasn't a child at all, that I was seventeen years old, the age at which my sister had married. He said again that I couldn't understand and that no young girl should go to the house of a man who is living with a woman that is not his wife. I went back home in a bad humour that evening, and as I undressed for bed I thought of how Giulio was always kissing me there in the woods, but he hadn't yet asked me to marry him. I was in a hurry to get married, but I wanted to enjoy myself afterward too. And perhaps with Giulio I shouldn't be so free. He might treat me the way his father treated his mother, shutting her up on the pretext that a woman's place was in the home, until she had turned into an old hag who sat all day long by the window, waiting for someone to go by.

Somehow I missed having Nini around the house, with his torn raincoat and his books and the lock of hair hanging over his forehead, telling me the way he always did that I ought to help my mother. Once, just to annoy Giulio, I went to see him. It was a Sunday afternoon and they served tea and cakes on an embroidered tablecloth and Antonietta kissed me on both cheeks and made a great fuss over me. She wore good clothes and painted her face, and she had blonde hair, wide hips, and narrow shoulders. Her children were there, too, doing their homework, and Nini sat listening to the radio instead of reading a book the way he used to do at home. They showed me the whole apartment, the bedroom and bath and the potted plants all over. The place was neater and cleaner than Azalea's. We talked about one thing and another, and they told me to be sure to come again.

Nini walked back with me part of the way, and I asked him why he didn't come home. I began to cry and told him it was worse than ever there without him. He sat down on a bench with me and stroked my hands and told me not to cry or else the mascara would run off my eyelashes. I told him that I didn't paint myself up like Antonietta, who looked like a perfect fright, and that he'd do a lot better to come home. The best thing of all, he said, would be for me to get a job and come and live in the city, and then he'd take me to see the films. But the point was for me to earn my own living and be independent. I told him he might just as well put that idea out of his head because I didn't have the slightest intention of doing anything of the sort. I was going to marry Giulio and come and live in the city with him, because he didn't like the country either. And that was how we said good-bye.

3

I told Giulio that I'd been to see Nini, but this time he wasn't angry. All he said was that he was sorry to see me do something that displeased him. I told him about Antonietta and her apartment, and he asked me if I'd like to have a little place like that of my own. Then he said that when he'd taken his medical degree we'd get married, but it wasn't possible any sooner. Meanwhile, he said, I shouldn't be so hard on him.

'I'm not hard on you,' I answered.

Then he asked me to go with him the next day to Fonte Le Macchie. This was a long walk, a large part of it uphill, and I was afraid of snakes.

'There aren't any snakes up that way,' he said. 'And we'll eat blackberries and stop for a rest whenever you are tired of walking.'

I pretended not to see what he was driving at and said Giovanni might come with us, but he said that he wanted us to be alone together without Giovanni tagging along. We never got all the way to Fonte Le Macchie, because at a certain point I sat down on a rock and swore I wouldn't go a step farther. He tried to scare me by saying he could see a yellow snake beating around under the bushes. I told him to let me alone, because I was tired and hungry, and so he pulled some provisions out of a bag. He had a couple of flasks of wine with him, too, and made me drink so much of it that finally I lay down in a daze and he did exactly what I had expected.

It was late when we started home, and I was so tired that I had to stop at every other step. When we reached the beginning of the woods he said he'd have to run on ahead or else his mother would wonder why he hadn't come home. He left me alone and I stumbled back in the darkness, with a pain in my knees. Azalea came to the house the next day and I went part of the way home with her and told her what had happened. At first she thought I was bragging and didn't believe me, but suddenly she stopped and said abruptly:

'Is that true?'

'Yes, it's true, every word of it, Azalea,' I said, and then she made me tell her the whole story again. She was so worried and angry that she tore the buckle off her belt and said she would tell her husband to speak to my father about it. I told her not to and added that there was plenty I could tell about her if I chose to. We exchanged quite a few hard words, and the next day I went to the city to make peace with her.

She had calmed down over-night, and I found her cutting out a dress to wear to a dance to which she had been invited. She told me I could do what I damn well pleased as long as she didn't have to be bothered about it, but she thought the doctor's son was a vulgar fellow and didn't care for him at all.

On the way home I met Giovanni with Nini and Antonietta and we went for a dip in the river, all except Antonietta, who stayed in the boat because she didn't know how to swim. I swam up and jiggled the boat as if I were going to turn it over, but then I began to feel cold and climbed in and started to row. Antonietta told me about her husband and the illness he had died of and the debts and lawsuits he had left behind him. I was bored with her story and thought how funny she looked, sitting in the boat as if she were making a formal call, with her pocket-book and hat on her lap and her knees held close together.

That evening Giovanni came into my room and said he was in love with Antonietta. He paced up and down the floor, saying that he didn't know how he'd ever get over it and asking me whether or not he should tell Nini. I was very impatient with him and told him that I'd had enough of all these love stories and I only wished he and Nini and Azalea would let me alone.

'It was a bad day when you were born,' he said, and went out, slamming the door behind him.

4

Giulio said I should go swimming in the river with him and have some fun afterward in the city. So we went for a swim and ate some ice-cream and then he took me to a hotel called the Moon. The hotel was at the end of a solitary street. With its drawn blinds and deserted garden it looked like a private house whose owners had gone away, but the rooms had mirrors and wash-basins and rugs on the floor. I told

Azalea about going to the hotel and she said that sooner or later I was going to get myself in trouble. I didn't see Azalea very often just now because she had taken up with a new lover, a penniless student, for whom she was always buying gloves and shoes and things to eat.

One evening my father burst into my room, threw his raincoat on the bed, and said:

'I told you that I'd smash your face for you.'

He took me by the hair and began to hit me, while I cried:

'Help! Help!'

Finally my mother came, with her apron full of potatoes, and said:

'What's the matter? What are you doing, Attilio?'

'This is the last straw,' said my father. He turned quite pale as he sat down and ran his fingers through his hair. I had a bleeding lip and red marks on my neck and I was so dizzy that I could hardly stand up. My mother wanted to help me wipe away the blood, but my father took her by one arm and pushed her out of the room. Then he followed her, leaving me alone. His raincoat still lay across my bed, and I picked it up and threw it down the stairs.

While the rest of them were at supper I crept out the front door. The sky was clear and starry. I was trembling with cold and fright, and the blood dripping from my lip had run down over my dress and stockings. I set out toward the city, but I was uncertain as to where I should go. I thought first of Azalea, but her husband would have stormed me with questions and reproaches, so I went to Nini instead. They were all sitting around the dining-room table, playing parcheesi. The children took one look at me and screamed. I threw myself down on a couch and began to cry. Antonietta brought an antiseptic to put on my lip, gave me a cup of camomile tea, and set up a cot for me in the hall.

'Tell us what happened, Delia,' said Nini.

I told him that my father had attacked and tried to kill me because I was going with Giulio and that they must find me a job in the city because after this I couldn't live at home.

'Get undressed and go to bed,' said Nini, 'then I'll come and talk to you about what to do.'

They all went away and I put on a lavender nightgown belonging to Antonietta and slipped into the cot. After a while Nini came and sat down beside me.

'If you like I can find you a job in the factory where I work. You'll find it hard going at first because you've grown into a big girl without ever lifting a finger. But you'll get used to that. If I can't find you anything there you'll have to do housework.'

I told him that I'd rather work in the factory than do housework any day. But why couldn't I sell flowers on the steps of the cathedral?

'Don't be silly,' he said. 'You don't know enough arithmetic to sell anything.'

Then I said that Giulio was going to marry me as soon as he had his degree.

'Put that notion out of your head,' he said. And he told me that Giulio was engaged to a girl in the city, whom everyone knew, a thin girl who drove her own car. I started to cry again, and Nini told me to go to sleep and brought me an extra pillow.

The next morning I got dressed and went out early with Nini into the cool and empty city. He went with me as far as the outskirts and we sat down near the river until it was time for him to report to work. He said that every now and then he felt an urge to go to Milan and look for a job in a bigger factory.

'But you'd have to shake off Antonietta,' I said.

'Of course. You can't see me taking her and her two brats and her stationery shop along, can you?'

'Then you don't love her?' I said.

'Oh, I love her after a fashion. We'll stick together just as long as we like it, and then we'll call it quits without any ill feelings on either side.'

'Then turn her over to Giovanni, who's crazy about her,' I said.

He started to laugh. 'Giovanni? Antonietta's not so bad, you know. She makes faces every now and then, but that's not serious. Only I'm not in love with her.'

'Who are you in love with, then?' I asked, and it flashed across my mind that he might be in love with me. He looked at me and laughed and said:

'Does everybody have to be in love? It's possible not to love anyone and to put one's mind on other things.'

I had on a thin dress and my teeth were chattering.

'You're cold, little girl,' he said, taking off his jacket and throwing it around my shoulders.

'How affectionate you are!' I said.

'Why shouldn't I be affectionate with you? You're so unlucky that it's really a shame. Don't think I don't know that you've got yourself into a mess with that Giulio. Azalea told me, but I know you well enough and I had guessed as much already.'

'It's not so,' I said, but he told me to be quiet because he knew better.

Just then the whistles blew and Nini said that he had to go to work. He wanted me to keep his jacket, but I refused because I should have felt funny meeting anyone with a man's jacket around me.

'Why don't you come back home, Nini?' I asked when we said good-bye.

He promised to come and see me the next day, which was Sunday. Then he leaned over abruptly and kissed me on one cheek. I stood still, watching him go away with even steps, his hands in his pockets. I was astonished that he should

23

have kissed me, something he had never done before. I walked slowly along, thinking of how Nini had kissed me and how Giulio was engaged to a girl in the city of whom he had never said a word. 'People are strange,' I said to myself. 'You never can make out what they want.' And then I thought how my father might be at home and hit me again, and this made me feel very sad. But my father pretended not to see me and didn't say a word, and neither did any of the rest of them.

The next day Nini came in a state of great excitement, saying that he had found me a job. Nothing doing at the factory, but there was an eccentric old lady who wanted someone to go out with her every afternoon. I was to come to the city every day after lunch and go back home at night. The pay wouldn't be enough at the start for me to rent a room of my own, but she had promised to increase it very soon. The old lady was an acquaintance of Antonietta, and Antonietta had recommended me to her. That day there was no one in the house, and Nini and I lay out under the pergola and talked as peacefully as if we were beside the river.

'The river's the best, though,' said Nini. 'You must meet me there soon for a swim. You don't know how wonderful it is early in the morning. It's not too cold and it puts life into you.'

Then I asked him again with whom he was in love.

'Let me alone,' he said. 'Don't tease me to-day, when I'm so happy.'

'Tell me, Nini,' I insisted. 'I won't breathe a word to a soul.'

'What does it matter to you?' he answered. And he began to tell me to wash thoroughly and put on a dark dress when I went to the old lady. I told him I didn't have any dark dress and if he was so fussy I didn't want to go at all. Then he was angry and went away without saying good-bye.

5

I went to the old lady's house in my light blue dress and found her all ready to go out, with her hat on and powder smeared over her wrinkled face. I was to take her for a walk and make things agreeable for her, so her daughter told me, then bring her home and read the newspaper aloud until she was sleepy. I took very short steps, while she hung on to my arm and muttered the whole while about one thing and another. She said I walked too fast, that I was too tall for her, and reaching up to my arm was a strain. She shook all over when it came to crossing the street, and everyone turned around to stare. One day we ran into Azalea, who didn't have the slightest idea that I was working and gaped with astonishment.

When we went back to the house the old lady drank a cup of hot milk and I read the paper. Soon after that she began to nod and I was free to go. But I was often in a bad mood and got no enjoyment from being in the city. One evening I decided on the spur of the moment to go and meet Nini at the factory gate. He saw me from a distance and his face lighted up. But when he started to walk with me, dirty and tired as he was, and wearing an old, pale grey hat and down-at-the-heel shoes that were too large for him and dragged along the pavement, I was ashamed to be seen with him and began to be sorry I had come. He was quick to catch on and take offence and he became angry when I told him that the old lady bored me to death. But by the time we reached the river he had calmed down and told me that he had found a picture of Giovanni with a message scrawled on the back in one of Antonietta's bureau drawers.

'Perhaps it's all for the best,' he said.

'What do you mean, all for the best?'

'Why should I care?'

'You're a cold fish. I hate you.'

'Very well, then, I'm a cold fish. And what are you?' He looked at me for a minute and then said: 'You're just a poor little girl.'

'Why do you say that?'

'Is it true that you went to the Moon?'

'Who told you?'

'A little birdie told me,' he said. 'Have you been there more than once?'

'That's none of your business,' I said.

'Poor little girl! Poor little girl!' he said half to himself.

I was angry and clapped my hand over his mouth. He put his arms around me and threw me down on the ground, kissing my face and ears and hair.

'Are you crazy, Nini?' I said. 'What are you doing?' I was half laughing, half afraid. He sat up and pushed back his hair.

'See the kind you are? Any man can go as far as he likes with you.'

'Is that what you were trying to find out just now?'

'No. Forget it. I was only joking.'

Giulio was waiting for me on the road that evening.

'Where have you been all this time?' I asked him.

'In bed with a fever,' he said, trying to take my arm. But I told him to go away and leave me alone, because I knew that he was engaged to a girl in the city.

'What girl?' he asked.

'A girl who has a car of her own.'

He laughed and struck his knee with his hand.

'People are always telling tall tales,' he said. 'And you fall for them. Don't be a goose. Meet me in the woods to-morrow after lunch.'

But I told him that I wasn't free in the afternoon any more because of the old lady.

'Come in the morning, then,' he said.

I turned my face away because I was afraid that he might see that Nini had kissed me. The next morning in the woods he kept asking who had told me that he was engaged to a girl in the city.

'There are plenty of people who have it in for me,' he said. 'Sour grapes, most likely.'

He teased and teased me until I told him it was Nini.

'I'll tell Nini a thing or two when I see him,' he said. Then he began to tease me about my job of taking the old lady out for a walk.

I went again to meet Nini when he came out from work. But he was annoyed because the old lady's daughter had complained to Antonietta that I was always late.

'There's no counting on you,' he said. 'You won't get very far if you go on like this. It's just as well they didn't take you on at the factory.'

I said that I was sick and tired of the old lady and didn't want to have anything more to do with her.

'Keep on going until the end of the month and collect your pay,' he said. 'And give the money to your mother, so she can buy the boys some shoes.'

'I'll keep it, that's what I'll do,' I said.

'Good! Good girl! Don't think of anyone but yourself! Buy some glad rags and have a good time. What should it matter to me?'

He didn't want to go down by the river, and we walked along toward his house. We got there just as Antonietta was closing the shop. She was very angry and said that if she'd known me better she'd never have recommended me for the job. Now I'd put her in a very awkward position. They had told her that I always came late and went away early and when I read the paper I was always giggling and making mistakes, just to be funny. She barely nodded good-bye as she and Nini went into the house.

On my way home I was very low in my mind. I hadn't felt

well for several days, and the mere smell of food was enough
to make me lose my appetite. 'Do you suppose I'm pregnant?'
I thought to myself. 'What am I going to do?' I stood still
on the road, with my heart in my throat. The country was
silent around me, and I could see neither the city that I had
left behind me nor our house that lay farther along the way.
Other girls went to school, spent the summer at the shore, got
asked to dances, and chattered like so many magpies. Why
wasn't I one of them? Why wasn't my life like theirs?

When I got up to my room I lit a cigarette, but it had a bad
taste and I remembered that Azalea couldn't smoke either
when she was expecting her children. I must be pregnant, and
when my father found out he'd kill me. 'Perhaps it's just as
well,' I thought. 'Why not die and get it over with?'

But the next morning when I got up I felt calmer. The
sun was out and I picked grapes from the vines on the pergola
with the boys. Then I walked through the village with
Giulio. There was a fair on the street, and he bought me a
good-luck charm to hang around my neck. Every now and
then a wave of fright came over me, but I pushed it away and
said nothing. I enjoyed the sight of the fair, with chickens
clucking in their boxes and children blowing their horns.

Later I remembered that Nini had been angry with me and
decided to go and make up with him. Because it was a holiday
Nini had not gone to work, and I found him just as he was
coming out of the café. He asked me if I wanted a drink, and
I could see that he was no longer angry. I said no, and we
went down by the river.

'Let's be friends,' I said after we had sat down.

'All right. But in a few minutes I've got to go home.'

'Can't I come too? Is Antonietta still angry?'

'Yes. She says you never even thanked her for what she
did. And she's jealous too.'

'Jealous of me?'

'Of you, yes.'

'I'm glad of that!'

'You would be glad, you little monkey! You love to see other people suffer. Now I've really got to go. But I don't want to.' He lay flat on the grass with his arms folded under his head.

'Do you like being with me? Better than with Antonietta?'

'Yes, I do. A whole lot better.'

'Why?'

'I don't know why, but I do.'

'And I like being with you too. Better than with anyone else.'

'Better than with Giulio?'

'Yes.'

'Now, how do you account for that!' he said, laughing.

'I really don't know,' I said. I wondered if he was going to kiss me, but there were too many people passing by. All of a sudden I saw Giovanni and Antonietta coming toward us.

'I was sure we'd find them here,' said Giovanni. But Antonietta eyed me coldly without saying a word. Nini stretched lazily and got up, and all four of us went for a walk in the city. That evening Giovanni said:

'What a funny girl you are! All of a sudden you're crazy about Nini and do nothing but hang around him.'

That was quite true. I waited to see him all day long and went to meet him every evening at the factory gate. When he and I were together I managed to forget my new fear. I liked him when he was talking and when he was silent, as he often was, biting his nails and thinking about something. I was always wondering when he would kiss me, but he never did. He sat some distance away from me, rumpling his lock of hair and then smoothing it down again, and then he said:

'Go on home.'

But I didn't want to go home. The only time I wasn't bored was when we were together. I liked to hear him talk about the books he was always reading. I didn't know what he was talking about, but I nodded my head and pretended to understand.

'I'll bet you haven't understood a word of what I just said,' he'd say, giving me a playful slap on the cheek.

6

One evening while I was undressing I suddenly felt as if I were going to faint and I had to lie down on the bed. At the same time I was shivering and covered with perspiration. 'Azalea used to be the same way,' I said to myself. 'I'll tell Giulio to-morrow. After all, he's got to know. But what will he say? What are we going to do? Can it really be true?' I knew very well that it was. I was so hot that I couldn't go to sleep, so I threw the covers off and sat up in bed with my heart thumping. What was Nini going to think of me? Once I had almost told him, but then I had lost my nerve.

I saw Giulio in the village the next morning, but only for a minute, because he was going hunting with his father.

'You're not looking like much,' he said.

'I didn't sleep well,' I answered.

'I hope to shoot a hare,' he said. 'I feel just like going out in the woods.' He looked up at the clouds floating over the hills. 'It's good hunting weather,' he added.

That day I didn't go to the old lady's. I wandered about the city for a while and then went to see Azalea. She was out, but I found Ottavia ironing in the kitchen. She had on a white apron and shoes instead of bedroom slippers. The whole household was in better order when Azalea's personal affairs were running smoothly, and even the children seemed to have put on weight. While Ottavia ironed one of Azalea's brassières she told me that everything was all right and Azalea was very happy. The student was quite different from his predecessor. He never neglected telephoning her and he did whatever she asked; in fact, he had not gone to see his parents in the country on this particular day just because Azalea had told him not to. The main thing was that 'the master' should not catch on. They must be very careful. And Ottavia begged me to wait until Azalea came home and tell her how careful she must be. I waited for a while, but Azalea didn't come and so I went away. It was time for Nini to be coming out of the factory, but I walked slowly toward home. Rain started to fall and my feet got wet. As soon as I reached home I went to bed and slid away down between the sheets. I told my mother that I didn't feel well and wouldn't have any supper.

'A bit of a chill,' my mother said.

The next morning she came into my room, felt my forehead, and said I didn't have any fever. She told me to get up and help her scrub the stairs.

'I can't get up,' I said. 'I don't feel well.'

'So that's the game, is it?' she said. 'You're playing sick. I'm the one to be sick with all the back-breaking work I do. When mealtime comes around I'm too tired even to eat. And you enjoy seeing me die by inches.'

'I can't get up, I told you. I don't feel well.'

'What's the matter with you?' my mother asked, pulling down the sheet and peering into my eyes. 'Is anything wrong?'

'I'm pregnant,' I said. My heart was beating fast, and for the first time I was afraid of what my mother might do. But she showed no surprise. She sat quietly on the edge of the bed and pulled the blanket over my feet.

'Are you sure?' she asked.

I nodded and began to cry.

'Don't fret,' said my mother. 'Everything will come out all right. Does the young man know?'

I shook my head.

'You should have told him, little fool. But now we'll put everything straight. I'll go and talk to those thugs myself.

We'll have a thing or two to say to them.' She pulled her shawl up over her head and went out. Pretty soon she came back. Her face was red, but there was a satisfied look on it.

'The thugs,' she said. 'But it's done. Only we'll have to wait a while until the young man has taken his degree. They insist on that. Now it's a matter of keeping your father quiet. But I'll see to that. That's your mother's job. You stay in bed and keep warm.' She brought me a cup of coffee and then went to scrub the stairs. I could hear her laughing to herself, but a minute later she was standing in front of me.

'I like the boy well enough,' she said. 'It's the mother that rubs me the wrong way. The father saw reason from the start. He said he was willing to make good on his son's behalf as long as we didn't cause any scandal. He even asked me if I'd have something to drink. But the mother raised a terrible row. She threw herself on her son as if she were going to kill him and screamed like a slaughtered chicken. But that didn't discourage me. "My daughter's only seventeen," I said, "and the court will protect her." She turned white, sat down, and stroked her cuffs in silence. The boy hung his head and didn't look at me. The doctor was the only one to speak. He begged me for the sake of his position not to cause a scandal. He paced up and down the rug the whole time. If you could see the rugs they have! And the house! They've everything.'

I turned my head to one side as if I wanted to sleep, in order to make her go away. After a while I really did fall asleep and didn't wake up until my father came in. I pricked up my ears and heard him talking to my mother in their room. All of a sudden he raised his voice and I thought :'Now he's coming to kill me!' But he didn't. Giovanni came instead.

'Nini told me to ask why you didn't come yesterday and tell you he's expecting you to come to-day.'

'Can't you see I'm in bed?' I answered. 'I'm not well.'

'Scarlet fever, that's my guess,' he said. 'There's an

epidemic, and Antonietta's children are both down with it. Soon your face will look like a big strawberry.'

'I haven't got scarlet fever,' I said. 'It's something quite different.'

He didn't ask any questions but looked out the window and said:

'Where's he off to now?'

I looked out the window, too, and saw my father walking toward the village.

'Where can he be going?' repeated Giovanni. 'He hasn't even had lunch.'

Toward evening Azalea walked into the room with my mother.

'We're going to have a beautiful baby here next May,' said my mother.

Azalea didn't answer. She sat down sombrely and unhooked her fox fur.

'Mother's a great talker,' she said when we were alone, 'but it's not so certain that he'll marry you. When Father went to see them they raised the roof, and it's a wonder no one got killed. They offered Father money on condition that he would keep his mouth shut and you would go and have the baby somewhere far away. And said they'd see about the wedding later. Father shouted that they'd dishonoured him and that if Giulio didn't promise to marry you he'd take the whole thing to court. When he came to see me he was worn to a frazzle. I told you that's what would happen. Now you'll have to stick close to the house because in the village they're already beginning to talk. They can't possibly know anything, but they can smell it in the air. Well, it's your funeral.'

Later on Giovanni came back. He knew now what it was all about and looked at me with malice in his eyes.

'Nini doesn't know yet,' he said.

'I don't want you to tell him,' I said.

'Don't worry about that. Do you think I want to brag

33

about your accomplishments? You've got yourself into a pretty mess! Who knows if he'll really marry you? Just now he's gone away, no one knows where. They say he was engaged, you know. Not that I care. You can go to the devil, you and your baby.'

I sat up and threw a glass that was on the night table at him. He screamed and started to hit me, but then my mother came in, took him by the collar of his jacket, and hauled him away. My mother didn't want me to go near the kitchen or any of the downstairs rooms, for fear I'd run into my father. Giovanni told me that my father had sworn he wouldn't come home if he had to see me. Anyhow, I didn't want to leave my bed. I put my dress on in the morning in order to keep warm, but then I lay on the bed with a blanket over me. I felt worse every day. Mother brought me my meals on a tray, but I hardly touched them. One evening Giovanni threw a book on my bed.

'That's from Nini,' he said. 'He waited three hours for you at the factory. He's been waiting there for days, so he told me. So I said you weren't well.'

I tried to read the book but never got more than halfway through it. There were two men in it who killed a girl and trussed her up in a suitcase. The story frightened me and I wasn't used to reading. I'd no sooner read a few pages than I forgot what had gone just before. I wasn't like Nini that way. But all the same, time went by. I had them bring the gramophone up to my room and listened to the hoarse voice singing:

'Velvety hands, your sweet perfume . . .'

Was the singer a man or a woman? It was hard to tell. But I was used to the voice and enjoyed hearing it. No other song could have pleased me half as well. I no longer wanted anything new. Every morning I put on the same old worn dress with patches all over it. Dresses now meant nothing to me at all.

7

When Nini turned up quite unexpectedly, while my mother was at church on Sunday, I was almost sorry to see him. I stared at the flowers, dripping with rain, that he had brought with him and his dripping hair and smiling face as if they were unfamiliar and extraneous.

'Shut the door,' I said angrily.

'Did I startle you? Were you sleeping? I've brought you some flowers,' he said, sitting down near me. 'How do you feel? Better? What was it, anyhow? You have such a funny look on your face.'

'I'm not well,' I answered, realizing that he still didn't know.

'Your face is thin and you've lost all your colour,' he said. 'It's a very poor idea to stay shut up in your room. You ought to get some exercise. I've been waiting for you at the factory gate. Every day I think: "Perhaps she's better now and will come." Will you come to meet me there again when you get well?'

'I don't know.'

'What do you mean, you don't know? Why that high-and-mighty tone of voice? You've lost your good disposition too. Will you come or won't you?'

'They won't let me go out,' I answered.

'What's that? Why not?'

'They don't want me to go around with Giulio. Or with you either. Or with any boy.'

'All right,' he said, 'have it your own way.' And he began to pace up and down the floor. 'That's all lies,' he said suddenly. 'It must be a tricky way you've thought up of sending me to the devil. How you like to see me suffer, don't you? I'm no good for working or for anything else. I think of you all day long. That's what you wanted, isn't it? To break up my life completely.' He looked at me with hard, wet eyes. 'Well, you've got what you want, then.'

'I don't particularly want to see you suffer,' I said, sitting up in bed. 'Perhaps I did once upon a time. But not now. I've other things on my mind. I'm going to have a baby.'

'Oh, is that it?' he said, without showing very much surprise. But his voice went flat and dull. 'Poor little girl!' he said, laying a hand on my shoulder. 'What will you do?'

'I don't know,' I said.

'Is he going to marry you?'

'I don't know. I haven't the slightest idea. They've gone to talk to him about it, and it seems he may marry me after he gets his degree.'

'I love you. Do you know that?' he said.

'Yes,' I said.

'You might have come to love me too, after a while,' he said. 'But there's no point in talking about that now. It would just make it hurt all the more. That's all over. Here I am beside you and I don't know what to say. I'd like to do something to help you, and at the same time I wish I could go away and never hear your name again.'

'Go along, then,' I said, starting to cry.

'I was terribly happy,' he said. 'I thought that little by little you'd fall in love with me too. At least, sometimes I thought so. At other times I was afraid I loved you too much. "She'll never love me," I said to myself; "she only likes to see people suffer. . . ." How silly we were, both of us.'

We fell silent, and tears streamed down my face.

'Perhaps he'll marry me when he gets his degree,' I said.

'Yes, perhaps he will. Besides, I'm not your type. You'd take it out of me. We're too different.'

And Nini went away. I heard him go down the stairs and stop in the garden to speak to my mother. Then my mother came up to see me and said that she'd seen the doctor's family at church, but Giulio wasn't there. The doctor had told her that he'd sent Giulio to the city and asked her if he could come to see her at the house.

'That means it's in the bag,' my mother said.

The doctor came that very day, and he and my mother shut themselves up in the dining-room and talked for nearly two hours. Then my mother came upstairs and told me to be glad, because it was settled that we were to get married in February. Until then Giulio had to have peace and quiet and concentrate on his studies and we weren't to see one another. In fact, the doctor wanted me to leave the village at once in order to avoid the possibility of gossip. My mother had decided to send me to my aunt, who lived in a village higher up in the mountains, but not very far away. She was afraid that I might refuse to go, so she spoke in the highest terms of her sister-in-law, glossing over the fact that they had hardly spoken for years on account of a dispute over some furniture. She told me about the garden in front of my aunt's house, where I could walk to my heart's content.

'I hate to see you shut up in your room,' she said. 'But people have evil tongues.'

Later Azalea came, and she and my mother decided on the day when I was to leave. My mother wanted her to persuade her husband to lend us a car from the company he worked for, but Azalea wouldn't do it.

8

When I finally did go to my aunt's it was in a wagon. My mother went with me, and we drove through the fields so that no one should see us. I had on one of Azalea's coats because none of my own clothes fitted me any more. It was evening when we got there. My aunt was a stout woman with bulging black eyes and wore a pair of scissors around her neck because she was a dressmaker. The first thing she did was to quarrel with my mother over the amount of board I was to pay. Santa, her daughter, brought me something to eat and lit the fire. She sat down beside me and told me that she, too, hoped to get married some day, but 'there wasn't any hurry.' She laughed as she spoke, because she had been engaged for eight years to the mayor's son, who sent her postcards from the camp where he was doing his military service.

My aunt's house was a large one, with cold, empty, high-ceilinged rooms. There were sacks of corn and chestnuts all over the place, and strings of onions hung from the ceilings. She had had nine children, but gradually they had died or moved away, all except Santa, the youngest, who was now twenty-four. My aunt couldn't bear her and bawled her out all day long. Santa's marriage had been so long delayed chiefly because my aunt, with one excuse and another, wouldn't let her put a trousseau together but preferred to keep her at home and torment her. Santa was thoroughly scared of her mother, but whenever she spoke of leaving her in order to get married she burst into tears. She was surprised that I didn't cry when my mother went away, because she worked herself up into a state of despair every time her mother went to the city for only a day. Santa herself had been to the city only two or three times in her whole life and said she liked it better at home. And yet their village was worse than ours. It was pervaded by the smell of manure and unwashed babies squatting on the stairs. There was no electric light in the houses, and all the water came from a public fountain. I wrote to my mother to come and take me away because I didn't like it. She wasn't much good at writing letters, and so instead of answering she sent word through a coal dealer that I should stay put and make the best of it because there was nothing else to do.

And so I stayed on. I was not to be married until February and now it was only November. Ever since I had told my mother about the baby my life had taken a strange turn and I had to hide myself as if there were something shameful about me that no one should see. I thought back to the life I had led before, to the city where I had gone almost every day and the road I had travelled for so many years in every kind of weather. I remembered every inch of it, the heaps of stones, the hedges, the sharp turn revealing the river, and the crowded bridge that led directly to the central square. There in the city I had eaten salted almonds and plates of ice-cream and looked at the shop-windows. There was Nini coming out of the factory, Antonietta scolding the clerk who helped her in the shop, and Azalea waiting to go to the Moon with her lover. Now I was far away from all these things and recalled them with astonishment. Meanwhile Giulio was down there studying medicine, without coming to see me or even writing me a letter, just as if he had forgotten my existence and the fact that we were soon to be married. I hadn't laid eyes on him since he had found out that I was having a baby, and I wondered what he was thinking. Was he happy or unhappy over the prospect of marrying me?

I spent my days sitting in my aunt's kitchen, holding the fire tongs in my hands and thinking the same things over and over again. I wore a wool shawl over my shoulders and held the cat on my knees to keep warm. Every now and then women of the village came for a fitting, and my aunt, with her mouth full of pins, argued with them over the shape of a neck or a sleeve. When the countess was still alive, she said, she had gone every day to her house. The countess had been dead for some time now and her house had long since been sold, but my aunt still wept when she spoke of her.

'It was a pleasure to run those silks and laces through one's hands,' she said. 'The countess was very fond of me indeed. "My dear Elide," she used to say, "you'll never want for anything as long as I'm alive."'

But it seemed that the countess died poor because her husband and children had wasted her fortune.

The women who came to my aunt's stared at me with ill-concealed curiosity, and my aunt told them that she had taken me in out of sheer pity when my own family had thrown me out of the house on account of my misfortune. Every now and then one of them would start to moralize, but my aunt would cut her short, saying:

'What's done is done. And one can never tell. Sometimes when it looks most as if one had made a mistake everything turns out for the best. The girl may not look like much, but she picked on a fellow with money and education and he'll have to marry her. My daughter is the stupid one. She's been at it for eight years without getting herself married. She says it's all my fault because I won't give her a trousseau, but I say that his family's better off than I am and they can do something about it.'

'One fine day I'll come home pregnant, too, and then you'll be happy!' my cousin retorted.

'Just try it and you'll see!' my aunt said. 'I'll pull every one of your teeth out of your mouth if I hear you say that again. In my house such things don't happen. Five of my nine children are girls, but I've brought them up so well that no one's ever been able to say a word against them. Say again what you just said, you little devil!' she concluded, turning to Santa. Santa burst out laughing, and all the women joined her. Finally my aunt laughed, too, and they went on that way for some time.

This aunt was my father's sister. Although she hadn't set foot in our village for years she spoke about my family and their affairs as if she had an intimate acquaintance with them. She had it in for Azalea because she was stuck-up.

'Just because she wears furs in the winter she thinks she's somebody,' she said. 'The countess had three fur coats, you know, and she tossed them into the butler's arms when she came into the house as if they were so many rags. But I know furs and I can tell you how much they cost.

Azalea's is rabbit; anyone can smell the rabbit in it a yard away.'

'Nini's a queer one,' she said once. 'He's related to me almost as closely as you are, but I've never had a chance to know him. I met him in the city one day, and he bowed very politely and went his way. And yet I used to carry him in my arms when he was a baby and later on I patched his trousers. I hear that he's living with some woman or other.'

'He's working in a factory,' I said.

'Well, it's a good thing that one of you is working. My boys have always earned their living, but in your family no one does a thing. It's pathetic the way you've all grown up like weeds. You haven't made your bed once since you've been here. You sit in the kitchen all day with your feet on a stool.'

'I don't feel well,' I said. 'I'm not up to doing anything.'

'You have only to look at her to see that,' Santa interposed. 'Her face is as yellow as a lemon, and she's always twisting her lips with pain. Not everyone's as strong as we are. We're country people, and she comes from near the city.'

'From the city, you might as well say,' observed my aunt. 'She's run away to the city ever since she was a little girl, and that's how she lost all shame. No girl should go to the city unless her mother goes with her. But her mother's got more than one screw loose too. She was a shameless creature as a girl herself.'

'If Delia gets married she'll be better off than any of us,' said Santa, 'and then she'll be stuck-up too, just like Azalea.'

'That's true. The day she marries, her troubles are over. Let's just wait and see. Everything may turn out all right. Who knows? Let's hope so.'

'When you're married I'll come and be your personal maid,' said Santa after my aunt had gone away. 'That is, if I don't get married myself. But when I marry I'll have to tie a handkerchief around my head and go out and sweat in the fields all day on a donkey. My fiancé is a peasant and his family own land all around the village, and vineyards too. Not to mention their pigs and cows. I'll be well off myself, as far as that goes.'

'I wish you joy of it. Just to think of a life like that gives me a pain,' I said.

'Everything gives you a pain,' said Santa, cutting up a cabbage to put in the soup. 'I love Vincenzo and I'd love him just the same way if he were a beggar and I had to share his poverty. You can't even decide whether you love one man or another, because in your condition you've got to get married fast. And say thank you to the man that marries you. I don't mind hard work, if I can be near someone who loves me.'

We ate supper holding our bowls in our laps, without moving away from the fire. I could never manage to finish my soup, and my aunt would drink up what I left of it.

'If you go on eating so little you'll bring forth a mouse,' she said.

'It's sitting in the dark that frightens me and takes away my appetite. I feel as if I were in a tomb.'

'Oh, you need an electric light to eat by, do you? That's something new to me. Electricity makes for appetite, does it?'

After supper Santa and her mother stayed up for a while knitting woollen underwear. I was sleepy, but I stayed with them because I was afraid to go upstairs alone. We all slept in one big room under the attic. In the morning I was the last to get up. My aunt went down to feed the chickens, and Santa combed her hair and talked to me about her fiancé. I lay there listening with one ear and asked her to shine my shoes for me. She had to be careful that my aunt didn't catch her at it, because she was not supposed to wait on me. Meanwhile she went on talking.

'I'm no saint even if my name is Santa,' she said. And she

explained that she went walking with her fiancé when he came home on furlough and even let him kiss her.

Sometimes I walked in the garden, because my aunt said that a pregnant woman shouldn't stay seated too long and practically pushed me outside. The garden had a wall around it and a wooden gate leading on to the road, which I never bothered to open. I could see the village from our bedroom, and there was nothing inviting about it. I walked from the house to the gate and back to the house again, between a row of stakes for tomato vines and a row of cabbages. I was told to take care that I didn't step on anything.

'Watch out for the cabbages!' my aunt would call from the window.

The garden was full of snow and my feet were half frozen. What month was it and what day of the month? What were they doing at home, and was Giulio still in the city? I was quite in the dark. All I knew was that I was growing bigger and bigger, and twice my aunt had let out my dress. As my body grew bigger, my face became drawn and small. I looked constantly in the mirror and marvelled at how strange it had become. 'It's a good thing nobody can see me,' I thought to myself. I was humiliated by the fact that Giulio had not come to see me or written me a letter.

9

One afternoon Azalea did come, though. She was wearing her famous fur piece and an extravagant hat with three feathers on it. Santa was in the kitchen teaching some children to crochet, but Azalea went upstairs without a word of greeting and said she wanted to speak to me alone. She opened the first door she came to and walked in on my aunt, who had lain down to rest in a black petticoat, with her grey hair falling over her shoulders. When my aunt saw who it was she became nervous and excited and began to say all sorts of flattering things, as if she had forgotten the very uncomplimentary ones she had said in her absence. She wanted to go down and make some coffee, but Azalea said shortly that she hadn't time to drink it and preferred to spend the few minutes she could stay talking to me. After my aunt had gone away Azalea asked me how I was feeling.

'You're terribly large,' she remarked. 'It looks to me as if you'll be big as a house by your wedding day.'

She told me that Giulio's father had come to the house again and offered my mother money if she would let him out of the marriage. My mother had made a terrible racket, and he had gone away protesting that they had misunderstood him and that he was very happy about the whole thing. Then she said that I was to stay at my aunt's after the wedding, until the baby was born, so that there wouldn't be gossip in the village. Giulio's mother was a terrible miser, she said. She didn't give her servant enough to eat and she counted her sheets every day for fear they might be stolen. If I had to live with her it would be no joke.

'But Giulio says we'll have a place of our own in the city.'

'Here's hoping you do. Otherwise God help you.'

'Tell Giovanni to come and see me,' I said.

'I'll tell him, but I don't know whether he'll do it. He's tied up with a woman most of the time.'

'Antonietta?'

'No. I don't know who she is. A blonde that used to go around with Nini. They walk around the city arm in arm. But she's not so young, and I don't think much of her.'

'Ask Nini to come too. I'm bored here alone.'

'I haven't seen Nini for quite a while, but if I have a chance I'll tell him. And I'll try to come again myself, but I haven't much time. That fellow of mine is always after me. He whistles below my window in a way that's positively shameless.'

'Is it still the student?'

'Of course. You don't think I have a new one every month, do you?' she said sharply, pulling on her gloves. 'Good-bye, I have to go.' She put her arms around me and, somewhat in a daze, I kissed her cold, powdered face. 'Good-bye!' she called again from the stairs. And I saw her walk stiffly away through the garden, with my aunt at her heels.

My aunt called me to come and taste some tarts she had just finished baking. She was still upset by Azalea's visit and told me that she had asked her for some old shoes for Santa and herself, which Azalea had promised to bring next time she came. The tarts were heavy and made me sick at my stomach. Somehow Azalea had depressed me. I was sorry that I had sent any message to Nini. What would he think of me if he were to come? I no longer recognized myself in the mirror. How quickly I had used to run up and down the stairs! Now I could hear my clumsy footsteps echo through the whole house.

Giovanni turned up a few days later, riding a motor-cycle which had been lent to him by a friend. As soon as he got off he showed me a new watch and told me he had bought it with his commissions.

'What are commissions?' I asked.

Then he explained how he had been instrumental in the sale of a delivery van and found himself with a neat sum of money in his pocket.

'It's idiotic to break your back working eight hours a day in a factory like Nini. If you just have the gift of gab money will come easy. Nini gets so dog-tired that all day Sunday he shuts himself up in his room and sleeps. Besides, he's taken up drinking again, worse than before.'

'Do you see him often?' I asked.

'Not very. He's moved, you know.'

'Isn't he living with Antonietta?'

45

THE ROAD TO THE CITY

'No.'

I wanted to ask more about Nini, but he started in talking again about the commission he had earned on the delivery van and another that he expected to cash in on very soon. He sat in the kitchen with Santa and helped her shell chestnuts, while he went on bragging about his commissions and the idea he had of buying a motor-cycle of his own as soon as he had the money. Santa went out to church and we were left alone by the fire.

'Are you fairly happy up here?' he asked.

'I'm bored,' I said.

'Giulio's living in town. Antonietta and I ran into him in a café and he bought us a drink. He said that he was studying day and night and didn't have time to write to you.'

'Was Nini along?'

'No, Antonietta and he aren't speaking to one another. Antonietta says that Nini behaved very badly, that he pulled out of the house one fine morning shouting as if he were possessed by the devil. Now he has a furnished room piled high with all his books, and when he leaves work he shuts himself up in there to read and drink. When I go to see him he hides the bottle. He doesn't bother to buy food and he's unbelievably dirty. I took some books to him that he had left behind at Antonietta's. "You can have Antonietta," he said to me. "Go and take my place with her and you'll be better off than you are at home. Antonietta's a really good cook and her roasts are simply delicious."'

'And are you going to take him up on it?'

'I'm not a fool,' said Giovanni. 'If I did I'd end up having to marry her. I'll go with her as long as it suits me and then I'll leave her cold the way he did. When she hasn't any make-up on she shows her years. And she's always complaining about something.'

Giovanni stayed to supper and scared Santa with a ghost story. Then she went out with him in the garden.

46

'So long,' he said as he got on the motor-cycle. 'Keep smiling. When you get rid of that coconut of yours I'll take you and Antonietta to the films. There's nothing they don't show. Antonietta and I go all the time because she knows a man who owns a theatre and he gives us cut-rate tickets.' And off he went, with a loud noise, and a cloud of smoke.

Santa and her mother talked all evening long about Giovanni's ghost and one of their own, the figure of a nun which Santa herself had seen at the fountain. They got me so scared that I couldn't sleep. I tugged at Santa's arm, but she only muttered and turned over. I got up and walked with bare feet over to the window, thinking of Nini drinking alone in his room with his hair all rumpled and hiding the bottle when Giovanni came in. I wished I could talk to him and tell him I was afraid of ghosts and hear him tease me the way he used to do. But was he still such a joker? Perhaps he was slightly crazed with drink and didn't laugh as he did before. I began to cry uncontrollably, standing in my nightgown in the middle of the room. My aunt woke up, jumped out of bed, lit a candle, and asked what was the matter. I told her I was afraid, and she said to stop being silly and go back to sleep.

One day Santa's fiancé came for a furlough. He was tall and red-faced and too shy to talk. Santa asked me how I liked him.

'Not much,' I said.

'Perhaps a man has to have a moustache for you to like him.'

'No,' I said. 'I like men without moustaches too.' I thought of Nini and wished again that I could be far away from where I was now, lying with him beside the river in my light blue summer dress. I should have liked to know whether he still loved me. But I was so strange and ugly-looking at this point that I should have been ashamed to have

him see me. I was embarrassed enough by the presence of
Santa's fiancé.

10

Santa was angry with me because I told her I didn't like
her fiancé. She didn't talk to me for several days until I made
a formal apology because I needed her help washing my hair.
She heated the water and gave me a kiss when she brought it
in. She said that she didn't know what she would do without
me when I was gone and I must promise to write to her. The
sun was out and I went to sit in the garden with a towel over
my shoulders to dry my hair. All of a sudden the gate opened
and in walked Nini.

'How goes it?' he said. He was just the same as usual, with
his old raincoat, his hat jammed down over his head, and a
scarf thrown around his neck, but he had an absent and somewhat disagreeable look about him and I couldn't think of
anything to say. I couldn't bear to have him see me in this
condition. He told me to come and walk with him outside the
garden because he didn't want to have to talk to my aunt. I
took the towel off my shoulders and followed him outside,
and we walked among the stripped grapevines on the frozen
snow.

'How are things with you?' I asked.

'Not so good,' he said. 'Are you getting married in
February?'

'Yes.'

'Does Giulio come here often?'

'No, he's never been here at all.'

'Are you sorry that he doesn't come?'

I made no answer, and he stopped in front of me and looked
into my eyes.

'No, you're not sorry. You don't really care for him either.
Well, I ought to be glad. But instead it hurts me all the more.

48

It's all such a silly business. It's really not worth bothering one's head about.'

He stopped again, waiting for me to say something. Then he added:

'Do you know that I'm living alone?'

'Yes, I do.'

'To tell the truth, I like it. Whole days go by without my speaking to a soul. As soon as I get out of the factory I go back to my room and read without anyone to disturb me.'

'Have you a nice room?' I asked.

'No, not nice at all.'

I stumbled and he held me up with his arm.

'Perhaps you'd like to know whether I'm still in love with you. I think I'm not.'

'I'm glad,' I said, but it wasn't true and I felt very much like crying.

'When I came to see you the last time because they told me you were ill I meant to ask you to marry me. I don't know how such an idea ever came into my head. You'd have laughed or been angry at me, but one way or the other you'd have turned me down. Still I shouldn't have minded as much that way. What made me suffer was to know that you, you with your hair and voice, were going to have a baby, that your love for him might change your life and make you forget me entirely. My life will be just the same: I'll go on working at the factory and reading my books and bathing in the river when it's hot. Once upon a time I was almost happy. I liked to walk along the street and look at the women and buy books, and I thought about so many things that I imagined I really had some brains. I wish we two could have had a baby together. But I never told you I loved you because I was afraid. How silly it all was. . . . Don't cry,' he added, seeing tears in my eyes. 'It makes me angry to see you cry. I know you don't really care. You cry like that, but what does it really matter?'

'So I don't matter to you either?' I said.

'No,' he answered. It was beginning to get dark, and he took me back to the garden gate.

'Good-bye,' he said. 'Why did you send word for me to come?'

'Because I wanted to see you.'

'Did you want to see how I'd gone to the dogs? Well, I have, I can promise you that. All I do is drink.'

'You did that before.'

'Not the way I do now. Good-bye. I didn't tell you the truth just now when I said I didn't love you. That's not so. I still do.'

'Even ugly as I am?' I asked him.

'Yes,' he said, laughing. 'And you are ugly, all right Good-bye. I'm going.'

'Good-bye,' I said.

I found Santa weeping in the kitchen because Vincenzo had told her as he was going away that his family wouldn't let him marry her because they wanted him to marry a girl with more money. He had promised to marry her all the same, but her mother said that he'd never see it through. My aunt asked me where I had been, and I said, 'Out for a walk with Nini.'

'Oh, Nini. He might have spoken to me. I was with his mother when she died.'

Santa couldn't eat any supper.

'You're a silly girl,' her mother said. 'Why be in a hurry to get married? You've everything you need here at home. When a girl marries her troubles begin. Her children cry and her husband wants to be waited on and his parents make things all the harder. If you married Vincenzo you'd have to get up bright and early and go and work in the fields, because his people are only peasants. A fine occupation that would be. Girls don't know what's good for them. How could you be better off than staying here at home with your mother?'

'Yes, but later on?' said Santa, sobbing.

'What do you mean, later on? When I'm dead? Are you in such a hurry to see me die? I'll live to be ninety, just to spite you,' my aunt shouted, hitting Santa over the head with her rosary.

'With your cousin it's a different story,' she went on after a few minutes, while Santa dried her eyes. 'She had a piece of bad luck. I trust you haven't played any such tricks on me.'

'No, no, I swear I haven't.'

'Well, I hope not. But she may have set you a bad example and rotted you the way one piece of bad fruit rots another. You have no right to go out with a young man in the state you're in,' she added, turning to me. 'Never mind if you and Nini did grow up together. You can't expect everybody to know that.'

I didn't answer her but gave my attention to Santa.

'Don't worry,' I said to console her. 'As soon as I'm married I'll find a husband for you too.'

'Easy there,' said my aunt. 'Don't start crowing too soon. I've heard that your Giulio doesn't think of marrying you at all and still goes with a young lady in town. Several people have told me who have reason to know. How does it happen that he never comes to see you? Everyone else has come, even that wild Nini, but not he.'

'He has to study,' I said.

'Well, of course, I don't know about that. They've seen him with a young lady, that's what they tell me. You're here like a chicken, waiting for him to marry you, and he's put you quite out of his mind.'

'That not true,' I said.

'Go and ask him if it's not true, then. Tell him it's high time to marry you now that he's ruined your life this way. And if he doesn't do it soon you're going to talk. With men you've got to carry a big stick. You'll be in a pretty fix when you've a baby in your arms and have to earn a living. Because your father won't take you back, you can be sure of that.'

My aunt went away, leaving Santa and me alone.

'What an unlucky pair we are,' said Santa, attempting to embrace me and weep on my shoulder. But I didn't want to have her so near. I ran to the room upstairs and locked the door behind me. I stared into the darkness without crying and thought to myself that Giulio was quite right in not wanting to marry me. I had become downright ugly, even Nini said so, and then I didn't really care for him anyhow. 'The best thing I could do would be to die,' I said to myself, 'unlucky and stupid creature that I am. I don't even know what I want.' Perhaps what I wanted was to go back to old times, to put on my light blue dress and run away to the city and ask Nini if he was still in love with me. And to go into the woods with Giulio, too, so long as I didn't have to marry him. But all this was behind me, and there was no possible return. In fact, when I had been free to do all these things I had complained that my life was a bore and hoped for something unexpected to happen, such as marrying Giulio and going away from home for good. Now I remembered that it had often bored me to listen to him and that he had done all sorts of things to annoy me. I didn't really want to marry him at all. 'But what's the use?' I said to myself. 'We've got to get married at this point, or else I'm done for.'

My mother came to see me the next day and found me with a chill and fever which my aunt told her I must have caught when I went out walking with Nini late the previous evening. It was cold upstairs, and I was sitting in my usual place in the kitchen, with my legs practically in the fire. My teeth were chattering and yet I felt hot and feverish all over. My head was whirling and I could barely follow what my mother had to say. She was saying that there had been another scene with my father because Giulio had said that after all the baby might not be his.

'If you hadn't been such a little tramp,' said my mother, 'he wouldn't dare say anything of the sort.'

'That's very true,' said my aunt. 'Just yesterday she went out with Nini, and that's what's laid her low to-day. It doesn't matter to me, of course, except for the fact that she's staying in my house. If my daughter's reputation suffers, what am I to do?'

I told them to go away and leave me in peace because my bones ached. My aunt told my mother that if Giulio was wavering I should have a talk with him. My mother agreed and gave me his address in the city, which she had secretly obtained from the servant. Then she went away in a hurry in order to reach home before my father, who had forbidden her to visit me and told her he didn't even want to know whether I was dead or alive.

11

As soon as I felt better I decided to go down to the city. I took the money my mother had left for me and a box of cakes that my aunt wanted me to give to Giulio, but these I left with a woman sitting behind me. I was happy all the way, thinking of the various parts of the city that I hadn't seen for so long, looking out of the windows and listening to the chatter of the people getting on and off the bus. It was a lot more agreeable than my aunt's kitchen, and the mere fact of being in the company of people who didn't know anything about me or my troubles did a great deal to cheer me up. I was thrilled to see the city streets and arcades and looked hopefully around for Nini, but of course at that hour he was working. I spent all the money I had left buying some stockings and a bottle of Nocturne perfume. Then I went to Giulio's. The landlady, who limped and had a moustache, told me that he was asleep and she didn't dare wake him but that if I waited around for a while he would be sure to get up.

She took me into the parlour, pulled up the blinds, sat down beside me, and started to tell me all about her lame leg, how it had swollen up after she had fallen from a ladder, and what sort of care she was taking of it and how much it cost her. When she went out for a minute to talk to the milkman I took off my old stockings with holes in them, tucked them away in my bag, and put on the new ones. Then I waited for the landlady to call me.

When I went into Giulio's room he was still so sleepy that he didn't know who I was. He walked around in his stockinged feet, looking for his jacket and tie, while I turned the pages of some of the books on his table until he told me to leave them alone.

'What the devil got into you to make you come?' he said. 'I have a lot to do and I hate to waste time. And what are they going to say here in the house? I'll have to tell them who you are.'

'Tell them we're going to be married,' I said. 'Or don't you want to marry me any more?'

'Afraid I'll get away from you, are you?' he said angrily. 'Never fear, you've hooked me proper.'

'Listen here,' I said in a low voice that didn't seem to be mine, 'I know perfectly well you don't care a fig for me. I don't care for you either. But you've got to go through with the marriage or else I'll throw myself in the river.'

'You must have been reading cheap novels,' he said.

But all the same he was scared. He told me not to say silly things and called out to the landlady to make some coffee. Later he carried the cups away, locked the door, and said that there were better ways of passing the time than talking.

When I saw through the window that it was dark I said that probably I had missed the bus. He looked at his watch and told me to hurry up and get dressed because there was still a chance of catching it.

'I wouldn't know what to do with you to-night. If you

stayed in my room that old witch would shout it from the housetops.'

At the bus stop he was angry because I couldn't find my ticket, and when my handbag slipped down on the ground in the confusion my old pair of stockings fell out of it.

'You're just the same as you always were,' he said. 'You'll never know what it's all about.'

12

The night before the wedding I did nothing but cry, and my aunt insisted that I put cold compresses on my face so that no one would see the traces of my tears. She washed my hair with an egg and spread a cold cream that had once been a favourite with the countess over my chapped red hands. But I wept every time anyone opened their mouth and was a pitiful sight indeed, with my swollen eyes, trembling lips, and freshly washed and unruly hair.

My mother and father came early in the morning in a wagon, and my little brothers followed later, hopeful of getting something to eat. But they were so dirty that my aunt wouldn't let them go into the church. They didn't bring Giovanni with them because he had wisely run off to the city before it was time to go. Azalea was at the seashore, supposedly for the health of her children, but I gathered from a letter she wrote me that her lover was there and she couldn't be bothered to come. Last of all arrived Giulio and his father. Giulio wore a long overcoat, gloves, and highly polished shoes, which made him almost unrecognizable. My aunt had to borrow some chairs because her own were coming apart.

I didn't understand a word of what the priest was saying, and I was in mortal terror lest the smell of incense make me feel sick and faint. The church had just been whitewashed inside, and it was so bare and empty that it didn't seem like a church at all. My mother had brought a brazier to keep her feet warm, and my aunt had one eye on the door the whole time because she was worried about the dinner she had left in the oven. Santa wept because she was not the bride, and needless to say I wept without ceasing both at church and at dinner. The others pretended not to notice and talked among themselves about things that were of no concern to me.

When my father got up to go my aunt pushed me in front of him and told me to say I was sorry for all the trouble I had caused. He kissed me in an embarrassed fashion and turned his head away. He had changed a great deal in the last months and looked permanently hurt and sad. He was wearing glasses, and it was hard to believe that he had ever beaten me up on account of Giulio now that all the strength required for getting angry or shouting or beating anyone up seemed to have gone out of him. All through the festivities he had only shot me oblique glances, without ever saying a word, as if he were ashamed.

After dinner they all went away, leaving Giulio and me alone. We went upstairs together, and he told me that I was to stay at my aunt's until the baby was born. He would come to see me, he said, but not very often. Studying made him tired and I, too, should take it easy because having a baby was no joke. He told me to lie flat on the bed and rest after all the excitement of the wedding, while he went down to the kitchen where Santa was drying the dishes.

Giulio came again one Sunday to see me. He was dressed in his hunting clothes with the black boots and open jacket which I had seen him wear in the village. I asked him if he had found an apartment for us to live in.

'What do you mean, an apartment?' he said. 'I haven't even looked for one because my mother has already fixed up a room for us at home.'

'Oh, she has, has she?' I said in a voice trembling with rage. 'But I don't want to live with your mother. I'd rather die than be in the same house with her.'

'I won't allow you to talk that way,' he answered. And he said that he was going to rent an office in the city but that we would have to live with his parents because we hadn't enough money to take a place of our own.

'It would have been better not to get married in that case,' I said.

'It *would* have been better, there I agree,' he said. 'But I was sorry for you. Have you forgotten that you wanted to throw yourself in the river?'

I glared at him and went out through the garden without speaking to my aunt, who asked me where I was going. I walked for a long time, with my hands in my pockets and the wind in my face, among the grapevines where I had walked with Nini. When I came back Giulio had gone.

'You little wretch,' said my aunt, 'is that the way you behave with your husband? I heard you two quarrelling. It's too early for fights. A fine song and dance you'll lead him if you go on like that.'

A few days later Giulio came back with some yard goods for me to make myself some new clothes and said he would reconsider the idea of our living in the city.

'I'll stand up against my own family if it will make you happy,' he said. 'And you really don't deserve it because you're a bad girl.'

My aunt came to look at the materials, pulled out a fashion journal, and said that as soon as the baby was born she would make me something to wear. Giulio told her that he wanted me to go to a dressmaker in the city, and at that she grew red in the face and took offence. Finally she ordered us into the kitchen on the pretext of putting a closet in order.

'After all, this is my house,' she said.

Giulio said that if we were to live in the city I must dress in the proper style. And that didn't mean dressing like Azalea, who wore such extravagant things that everyone turned around to stare at her on the street. He didn't want me to be stared at, but it was important for me to be stylish if I wanted him to take me around. Santa teased him by saying that he had made a poor choice of materials because the colours were not in fashion.

'I expect I know what's in fashion better than you people here in the sticks,' Giulio retorted.

'Then why don't you dress like everybody else instead of wearing those ridiculous boots?' Santa asked him.

Both of them were put out, and Giulio began to talk to me as if we were alone. He said that if we lived in the city we'd have to entertain people every now and then, and this was one of the many things I'd have to learn how to do. Sometimes, he said, I seemed to him to have fallen from the moon. I looked at him to see if he was thinking of the Moon Hotel, that prostitutes' hangout, where he used to take me in the old days, but apparently he wasn't. He seemed to have forgotten all about the days before we were married and his reluctance to marry me and the fact that his father had offered me money if I would disappear along with our unborn child. Now he spoke often of the baby and how he imagined it would look and of a new kind of collapsible baby carriage that he had in mind to buy.

13

My labour pains came on at night. My aunt got up to call the midwife and sent Santa to her godmother's because she said it wasn't proper for a young girl to see how a baby is born. Santa was impatient to kiss the baby and give him a cap with pale blue ribbons that she had embroidered for him. Toward morning my mother arrived, bringing more caps and ribbons. By this time I was wild with pain and fear. I had two fainting spells and the midwife said they must take me to the hospital in the city. My mother wept all the way to the hospital, and looking into her face, I was sure I was going to die. I scratched my mother's hand and screamed at the top of my lungs.

The baby was a boy and they baptized him immediately for fear he wouldn't live. The next morning he was flourishing, while I felt very weak and had a fever, and they told me I couldn't nurse him. I stayed at the hospital a whole month, and the Sisters fed the baby with a bottle. Every now and then they brought him in for me to see, wearing Santa's cap on his head. He was ugly as sin, with long fingers, which he wriggled very slowly, and a secretive staring expression, as if he were about to discover something of importance.

The day after the baby was born my mother-in-law came to see me and scolded one of the Sisters for not binding him up the way she should. Then she sat stiffly on the edge of a chair with her pocketbook on her lap and a melancholy look on her long face and told me that in her time she had suffered a great deal more than me and the doctors had praised her for her courage. Against their advice she had nursed her baby and she had cried all day when she heard I wasn't going to nurse mine. At this point she pulled out a handkerchief and dried away her tears.

'It's sad for a baby to be denied his mother's breast,' she said. Then she pulled down my nightgown and said that I wasn't well enough developed to have milk, anyhow. I was angry and told her that my head ached and I wanted to sleep. She asked me if she had hurt my feelings, ran her fingers caressingly under my chin, and said that perhaps she had spoken too frankly. Then she pulled out a box of dates and put them under my pillow.

'Call me Mother,' she said as she went away.

When she had gone I ate all the dates, one by one, and put the box away, thinking it might be good to keep gloves in. I began to think of the white gloves with black stitching like Azalea's that I would buy as soon as I got out of the hospital,

59

and all the dresses and hats I had set my heart on, partly just
to annoy my mother-in-law and make her say that I was
wasting money. I was depressed by my mother-in-law's visit
and the prospect of having her hang around me.

When they brought in the baby and laid him beside me in
the bed I almost hated him because he seemed to look so much
like her. I was sorry to have a baby with my mother-in-law's
long chin and something of Giulio about him but not a trace
of myself. 'If I loved Giulio, I'd love the baby too,' I said
to myself, 'but this way it's out of the question.' Still there
was something about his soft damp hair and the way the
breath came and went in his little body that attracted me and
lingered in my thoughts after they had taken him away. He
didn't care in the least about what I thought of him or
whether I was happy or sad. He knew nothing of what was
in my mind or of the things I wanted to buy, and I was sorry
that he was still so small that I couldn't talk to him and tell
him what I was thinking. Then he sneezed and I pulled the
shawl up over him. Strange, I thought, how long he had lived
inside me, all the time I had sat in my aunt's kitchen and
when I had gone out walking with Nini. What had happened
to Nini, anyway? Why didn't he come to see me? But
perhaps it was just as well he didn't come because I was weak
and tired and talking made my head ache. Besides, Nini
would surely have said something nasty about the baby.

Giulio came to see me every evening, when the Sisters
were saying their prayers in the hall and a tiny lamp with a
silk shade was lit beside my bed. As soon as he arrived I began
to complain that I didn't feel well and that my whole body
ached as if it had been pounded into jelly. This was partly
true, but I said so mostly because I enjoyed giving him a
scare. I told him that I was sick and tired of the hospital and
the time never went by and some fine day I was going to run
away to the films. Then he would beg me to be patient and
make a great fuss and promise to bring me a surprise if I

stopped giving him so much worry. He was very tender and affectionate and said he'd do anything in the world to make me happy. In fact, he'd already rented an apartment in a building that had an elevator and every other possible convenience.

It wasn't true that I was unhappy at the hospital. I enjoyed myself there very much because I didn't have to lift a finger. Whereas after I left I would have to rock the baby to sleep and boil his milk and change his nappies all day long. As long as I was in the hospital I didn't know how to handle him at all and I was desperate every time he cried because he would get all red in the face and I thought he was going to burst. Occasionally, now that I had the money, I was impatient to get up, put on my clothes, look at myself in the mirror, and go out on the street. At times when I was bored like this there was nothing to do except to wait for someone to come and see me. My mother no longer came very often because she was busy at home and didn't want to come to the city in her shabby clothes. She didn't seem to be as satisfied with my marriage as she once was, and she had quarrelled with Giulio already over his refusal to lend her some money. My mother wouldn't forgive him and extended her grudge to me as well.

Azalea came to see me as soon as she returned from the shore. Her nose was peeling and she wore beach sandals. She wasn't getting on very well with her lover. He was jealous and wouldn't let her go to any dances, she said, and they fought tooth and nail most of the time.

'How's your son?' she inquired. I asked her if she wanted to see him, but she said she was fed up with children and tiny babies made her flesh creep.

'How are you making out with your husband?' she said. 'You were very wise to hold out for an apartment of your own. If you'd gone to live with his mother you'd never have a penny to call your own. You have to take a strong hand with the men because if you show any signs of weakness they'll strip the shirt off your back.'

The next day she brought her dressmaker to see me. I told her that I couldn't get out of my bed to have my measurements taken, but she said that the dressmaker was just coming to make my acquaintance and tell me about the latest styles. Then Azalea began to say that it was high time for me to get up. There wasn't a thing in the world the matter with me, she said; in fact, I was much stronger than she was.

It was a great occasion when I got up for the first time and slipped on a feathery pink wrapper that Azalea had brought me. I walked slowly down the hall on Giulio's arm, looking out the high windows at the street below. Who knows if Nini mightn't be passing by? I watched out for him every day. If I'd seen him on the street I'd have called down to him to come and see me and we should have talked and quarrelled as we did before. After all this time he couldn't possibly love me. But even if he did that was no reason for not coming to see me. Still my watch was all in vain and I grew ill-humoured and fought with the Sisters when they told me to go back to bed.

14

I found out the truth only when Giovanni came to see me, bringing a horn for the baby, as if he were already big enough to blow it. He was carrying a brief-case and said he was a travelling salesman for a wholesale draper. There was something nervous and evasive about his manner; he waved his arms in the air and didn't look at me when he spoke. 'He must be in some trouble,' I thought to myself. 'Perhaps Antonietta's left him.' Finally I asked him what it was.

'Nothing,' he said. But he rubbed his hands nervously as he walked up and down, and finally he stopped in front of the wall with his back to me.

'It's Nini,' he muttered. 'He's dead.'

I put the baby down abruptly.

'Yes, he's dead,' Giovanni repeated, starting to cry.

I fell back into a chair, feeling as if I couldn't breathe. Gradually Giovanni calmed down, wiped his face, and said that Nini had died some days ago, but they had told him not to let me know because I wasn't well enough to stand the shock. He had died of pneumonia, but Antonietta said it was all because of my cruelty. She said he had always been in love with me, even when he was living with her, and I had done nothing but tease him, even when I was pregnant by another man and knew I was going to be married. After that he had lost his head and begun to live like a savage, shutting himself up in a smelly room, without eating or sleeping, and getting drunk every day. If she ever ran into me on the street, Antonietta said, she'd tell me to my face what she thought of me. But Giovanni said none of this was true. Nini was a cold fish, he said, who cared more for drink than for women. He'd found him delirious in his bed one day and, thinking he was drunk, had poured a pitcher of cold water on his head, which Antonietta said had probably made him considerably worse. Because after that he had gone to call on Antonietta, and she had seen right away that he had pneumonia. She had called a doctor, and for three days she had kept hot mustard plasters on his back as the doctor told her, and she had cleaned his room and brought fresh sheets from her own house. But Nini breathed hoarsely and never came out of his delirium. He tried all the time to get out of bed, and she had to hold him down by force until he died.

When Giulio came to see me that evening I was walking up and down the room in tears and wouldn't go back to bed. The supper that the Sister had brought me lay untouched and cold on the table.

'What's the matter?' he asked.

'Nini's dead,' I said. 'Giovanni just told me.'

'Giovanni's a jackass! I'll settle with him!'

He felt my pulse and told me I had a fever and ought to lie down. I didn't answer and went on crying. Then he said that he was ashamed to have the Sisters see me standing there half naked, with my wrapper open down the front, and if I didn't look out I'd get pneumonia myself and follow Nini to the grave. His feelings were hurt because I didn't pay any attention, and finally, after he had telephoned to Azalea to come over, he sat down to read his newspaper without so much as looking up at me.

When Azalea came she told him to go out and get his supper and he went away, saying that he would leave us with our secrets, since obviously he was of no importance and we didn't need him around.

'He's jealous,' Azalea said. 'They're all the same.'

'Nini's dead,' I said dully.

'That's not exactly news,' she answered. 'I cried, too, when they told me. But later I thought maybe it was the best thing that could happen to him. I wish I were dead myself. I'm sick of being alive.'

'I caused him to die,' I said.

'You?'

'Yes, he was in love with me and I led him on just to see him suffer. After he heard I was marrying Giulio he lost interest in everything and shut himself up in his room and drank worse than before.'

Azalea looked at me incredulously.

'When someone's dead it's all very easy to imagine things. He took ill and died, that's all. You can't do anything about it and there's no sense in embroidering explanations. What did he care for you? He always said that he was sorry for you because you were such a silly girl and couldn't say no to the first man that came along.'

'He did so care for me,' I said. 'He was always taking me down by the river to talk. He read his books to me and told

64

me what they were about. And once he kissed me. I loved him too. Only I didn't know it and thought it was only that I liked to tease him.'

'Don't go mooning over Nini,' she said. 'One man's just like another. The thing to do is to have one around for company because it's too bad to be a woman alone. Nini wasn't as much of a fool as most of them, that's true, and his eyes were so bright that I can almost see them this minute. But even he was a bore in the long run, when you couldn't fathom what he was thinking. I'm not surprised he died, with all the cheap brandy he had in him. It's a wonder he lived as long as he did.'

When Giulio came back Azalea hurried away to cook her husband's supper because Ottavia had a toothache. That night I dreamed that Nini came to the hospital and ran away with the baby. I ran after him frantically, and he showed me the baby, about the size of an apple, in his coat pocket. All of a sudden Nini ran up a flight of stairs and Giovanni was with him, but when I called them there was no answer. I woke up breathless and perspiring and found Giulio standing beside my bed. He had come by early in the morning to see how I was feeling. So I told him about my dream.

'Nobody's run off with the baby,' he said. 'He's sleeping right here beside you and he won't be kidnapped, don't worry.'

But I went on saying that I had seen Nini big as life before me and he had held out his hand and spoken to me. I sobbed and tossed on my bed until finally Giulio told me to control my feelings and went away.

15

A few days later I left the hospital for my new apartment. This was the beginning of a different life. Nini was dead and there was no use thinking about him. Now I had Giulio and the baby, a houseful of new furniture and bright lights and my mother-in-law in person. The maid took care of the baby and I slept late every morning in the big double bed with the orange velvet cover. There was a bell beside me if I wanted to be waited on and a rug to put my feet on when I was ready to get up. I would walk around the apartment in my wrapper, admiring the wallpaper and the furnishings, running a brush slowly through my hair and drinking a cup of coffee. I thought back to my mother's house, with the mess left by the chickens all over the floor, the damp spots on the walls, and the little paper flaps fastened on to the lampshade in the dining-room. Was that incredible house still standing? Azalea kept saying we must go out there together, but I had no desire to do it. I was ashamed to think that I had ever lived there and I knew it would make me sad to see the room where Giovanni and Nini had slept together when we were all at home. When I walked about the city I stayed away from the river and sought out the most crowded streets where people could see me with my painted lips and new clothes. I looked at myself in the mirror half the day and thought no other woman had ever been so beautiful.

When my mother-in-law came she would shut herself up in the kitchen to question the maid about me, and I would listen at the keyhole. The maid told her that I didn't seem to care about the baby at all; I never picked him up when he was crying or asked whether he was eating properly. I was always sleeping or looking at myself in the mirror or going out for a walk, and she had not only to look after the baby but to do all the washing and cooking as well because I couldn't make so much as a cup of soup. My mother-in-law repeated these complaints to Giulio, but he said they were all poppycock. He always saw me with the baby in my arms, and there was no harm in my going out for a walk because I was young and he himself had told me to have a bit of fun. Giulio was so much in love with me that he paid no attention to his mother or anyone else. She told him that he was fat and stupid and couldn't see the truth even when it was staring him in the face. If I were unfaithful to him, she said, it would be no more than he deserved. But she didn't say anything to me because I scared her. She smiled and asked me to come and see her and stopped peering into my drawers because I told her to attend to her own business.

'When the baby's a little bigger,' I said to myself, 'and scoots around the house on a tricycle and asks me to buy him sweets and toys, maybe he'll be more fun.' But just now, with his big head on the pillow of his crib, he was very boring, and every time I looked at him I was annoyed and went out. It still seemed to me too good to be true to step out and find the city before me. Once I had walked over a dusty road, crowded with wagons, and arrived grimy and tired. Then when darkness fell and things were beginning to be lively it was time to go home. Now I would meet Azalea outside and we would sit in a café together. Little by little I came to live the same way Azalea did. I stayed in bed all day, got up in the late afternoon, made up my face, and went out with a fox fur thrown across my shoulders. As I walked I tossed my head and smiled in a provocative way, just like Azalea.

One day, on my way home, I ran into Antonietta and Giovanni walking arm in arm and bending over because it was raining and they had no umbrella.

'How do you do?' I said.

We went together to a café and I waited for Antonietta to jump on me and scratch my eyes out with her pointed red nails. She must have spent hours lacquering them, although it was hardly worth while because she had become so ugly and old. Instead of jumping on me she seemed actually afraid of what I might say and hid her feet under her chair when she saw me looking at them. She said that she had seen my baby in his carriage in the park and wanted to give him a kiss, but she did not dare go near him on account of the maid.

'You're lucky to have a servant,' she said. 'I have to do all my own work. But there isn't so much to do without a man in the house and myself alone with the children.'

She blushed, and red splotches came out on her neck. We looked at each other in silence, with the same thought in our minds. Then she asked me again about my husband and the baby and wanted to know whether I often went to dances and had a good time.

'You haven't been to see us at home,' said Giovanni. He said that things were just as usual and I was lucky to have got away. Then he asked me to lend him some money because although he had a good job my mother and father took all his salary.

They walked along with me and said good-bye at the door. While I was undressing in my room I thought of Giovanni walking home along the dark country road because he was afraid that if he stayed with Antonietta he'd end up by marrying her. All the time that we had sat at the café we had not said a word about Nini, as if we had forgotten how he used to like to sit crosswise on his chair and smoke and talk, propping his chin up on one hand and running the other through the lock that fell across his forehead. It was harder and harder to remember the way he looked and the things he used to say, and it frightened me to think of him now that he had receded far into the distance and become one of the vast multitude of the dead.

THE DRY HEART

'TELL me the truth,' I said.

'What truth?' he echoed. He was making a rapid sketch in his notebook and now he showed me what it was: a long, long train with a big cloud of black smoke swirling over it and himself leaning out of a window to wave a handkerchief.

I shot him between the eyes.

He had asked me to give him something hot in a thermos bottle to take with him on his trip. I went into the kitchen, made some tea, put milk and sugar in it, screwed the top on tight, and went back into his study. It was then that he showed me the sketch, and I took the revolver out of his desk drawer and shot him between the eyes. But for a long time already I had known that sooner or later I should do something of the sort.

I put on my raincoat and gloves and went out. I drank a cup of coffee at the counter of a café and walked haphazardly about the city. It was a chilly day and a damp wind was blowing. I sat down on a bench in the park, took off my gloves and looked at my hands. Then I slipped off my wedding ring and put it in my pocket.

We had been husband and wife for four years. He had threatened often enough to leave me, but then our baby died and we stayed together. Another child, he said, would be my salvation. For this reason we made love frequently toward the end, but nothing came of it.

I found him packing his bags and asked him where he was going. He said he was going to Rome to settle something with a lawyer and suggested I visit my parents so as not to be alone in the house while he was away. He didn't know when he'd be back, in two weeks or a month, he couldn't really say.

It occurred to me that he might never come back at all. Meanwhile I packed my bags too. He told me to take some books with me to while away the time and I pulled *Vanity Fair* and two volumes of Galsworthy out of the bookcase and put them in one of my bags.

'Tell me the truth, Alberto,' I said.

'What truth?' he echoed.

'You are going away together.'

'Who are going away together? You let your imagination run riot. You eat your heart out thinking up terrible things. That way you've no peace of mind and neither has anyone else. . . . Take the bus that gets to Maona at two o'clock,' he said.

'Yes,' I answered.

He looked at the sky and remarked: 'Better wear your raincoat and galoshes.'

'I'd rather know the truth, whatever it may be,' I said, and he laughed and misquoted:

'She seeketh *Truth*, which is so dear
As knoweth he who life for her refuses.'[1]

I sat on the bench for I don't know how long. The park was deserted, the benches were drenched with dew, and the ground was strewn with wet leaves. I began to think about what I should do next. After a while I said to myself, 'I should go to the police and try to tell them how it all came about.' But that would be no easy matter. I should have to go back to the day when we first met, at the house of Dr. Gaudenzi. He was playing a piano duet with the doctor's wife and singing dialect songs. He looked at me hard and made a pencil sketch of me in his notebook. I said it was a good likeness, but he said it wasn't and tore it up.

'He can never draw the women that really attract him,' said Dr. Gaudenzi.

[1] 'He seeketh Liberty . . .' (Dante, *Purgatory*, i, 71).

They gave me a cigarette and laughed to see how it made my eyes water. Alberto took me back to my boarding-house and asked if he could come the next day to bring me a French novel which he had mentioned in the course of the evening.

The next day he came. We went out for a walk and ended up in a café. His eyes were gay and sparkling and I began to think he was in love with me. I was very happy, because no man had ever fallen in love with me before, and I could have sat with him in the café indefinitely. That evening we went to the theatre and I wore my best dress, a crimson velvet given me by my cousin Francesca.

Francesca was at the theatre, too, a few rows behind us, and waved to me. The next day, when I went to lunch at the house of my aunt and uncle, she asked me:

'Who was that old man?'

'What old man?'

'The old man at the theatre.'

I told her he was someone who was interested in me but that I didn't care for him one way or the other. When he came back to the boarding-house to see me I looked him over and he didn't seem so very old to me. Francesca called everyone old. I didn't really like him, and the only reason I was pleased to have him come and call on me was that he looked at me with such gay and sparkling eyes. Every woman is pleased when a man looks at her like that. I thought he must be very much in love. 'Poor fellow!' I thought to myself, and I imagined his asking me to marry him and the words he would say. I would answer no, and he would ask if we could still be friends. He would keep on taking me to the theatre and one evening he would introduce me to a friend, much younger than himself, who would fall in love with me, and this was the man I should marry. We should have a lot of children and Alberto would come to call. Every Christmas he would bring us a big fruitcake and there would be a touch of melancholy in his enjoyment of our happiness.

Lying dreamily on the bed in my boarding-house room, I imagined how wonderful it would be to be married and have a house of my own. In my imagination I saw exactly how I should arrange my house, with dozens of stylish gadgets and potted plants, and I visualized myself sitting in an armchair over a basket of embroidery. The face of the man I married was constantly changing, but he had always the same voice, which I could hear repeating over and over again the same ironical and tender phrases. The boarding-house was gloomy, with dark hangings and upholstery, and in the room next to mine a colonel's widow knocked on the wall with a hairbrush every time I opened the window or moved a chair. I had to get up early in order to arrive on time at the school where I was a teacher. I dressed in a hurry and ate a roll and an egg which I boiled over a tiny alcohol stove. The colonel's widow knocked furiously on the wall while I moved about the room looking for my clothes, and in the bathroom the landlady's hysterical daughter screeched like a peacock while they gave her a warm shower which was supposed to calm her down. I rushed out on to the street and while I waited in the cold and lonely dawn for the tram, I made up all sorts of stories to keep myself warm, so that sometimes I arrived at school with a wild and absent look on my face that must have been positively funny.

A girl likes to think that a man may be in love with her, and even if she doesn't love him in return it's almost as if she did. She is prettier than usual and her eyes shine; she walks at a faster pace and the tone of her voice is softer and sweeter. Before I knew Alberto I used to feel so dull and unattractive that I was sure I should always be alone, but after I got the impression that he was in love with me I began to think that if I could please him then I might please someone else, too, perhaps the man who spoke to me in ironical and tender phrases in my imagination. This man had a constantly changing face, but he always had broad shoulders and red, slightly awkward hands and an utterly charming way of teasing me every evening when he came home and found me sitting over my embroidery.

When a girl is very much alone and leads a tiresome and monotonous existence, with worn gloves and very little spending money, she may let her imagination run wild and find herself defenceless before all the errors and pitfalls which imagination has devised to deceive her. I was a weak and unarmed victim of imagination as I read Ovid to eighteen girls huddled in a cold classroom or ate my meals in the dingy boarding-house dining-room, peering out through the yellow window-panes as I waited for Alberto to take me out walking or to a concert. Every Saturday afternoon I took the bus to Maona, returning on Sunday evening.

My father has been a country doctor at Maona for over twenty years. He is a tall, stout, slightly lame old man who uses a cherry-wood cane for walking. In summer he wears a straw hat with a black ribbon around it and in winter a beaver cap and an overcoat with a beaver collar. My mother is a tiny woman with a thick mass of white hair. My father has few calls because he is old and moves about with difficulty. When people are sick they call the doctor from Cavapietra, who has a motor-cycle and studied medicine at Naples. My father and mother sit in the kitchen all day long playing chess with the local vet and the tax collector. On Saturdays when I came to Maona I sat down by the kitchen stove and there I sat all day Sunday until it was time to go. I roasted myself there by the stove, stuffed with thick soups and corn meal, and did not so much as open my mouth, while between one game of chess and the next my father told the vet that modern girls have no respect for their parents and do not tell them a word of what they are doing.

I used to tell Alberto about my father and mother and the life I led at Maona before I came to teach in the city. I told him how my father used to rap me over the fingers with his cane and I used to run and cry in the coal cellar. How I used to hide *From Slavegirl to Queen* under my mattress to read at night and how, when my father and the tax collector and the maidservant and I used to walk down the road between the fields and vineyards to the cemetery, I had a violent longing to run away.

Alberto never told me anything about himself, and I fell into the habit of asking him no questions. It had never happened before that anyone should take such an interest in me and attribute so much importance to what I had felt and said in the coal cellar or on the road to the cemetery. When I went for a walk with Alberto or when we sat in a café together I was happy and no longer felt so alone. Alberto told me that he lived with his mother, who was old and ailing. Dr. Gaudenzi's wife informed me that she was a very rich but batty old woman who spent her time smoking cigarettes in an ivory holder and studying Sanskrit, and that she never saw anyone except a Dominican friar who came every evening to read her the Epistles of Saint Paul. On the pretext that she could not get her shoes on without hurting her feet she had not left the house for years, but sat all day long in an armchair, in the care of a young servant girl who cheated her on food bills and maltreated her into the bargain. At first I didn't mind Alberto's unwillingness to talk about himself, but later I was disappointed and asked him a few questions. His face took on an absent and faraway expression and his eyes were veiled with mist like those of a sick bird whenever I inquired about his mother, or his work, or any other part of his life.

He never said that he was in love with me, but he came regularly to see me, bringing me books and chocolates, and wanting to take me out with him. I thought he might be shy and afraid to speak up, and I waited for him to say that he loved me so that I could tell Francesca. Francesca always had so much to tell and I never had anything. Finally, although he still hadn't spoken, I told Francesca all the same. That day he had given me some tan kid gloves and I was sure that he must love me after all. I told her that he was too old for me to marry, although I didn't really know how old he was— forty, perhaps—while I was only twenty-six. Francesca told me to get rid of him, that she didn't like his looks, and that I should throw the gloves back in his face because the snaps at the wrist were long since out of style and made me look like a country bumpkin. She'd always suspected, she said, that this fellow would bring me trouble. Francesca was only twenty at the time, but I respected her common sense and always listened to what she had to say. But this time I didn't listen. I liked the gloves in spite of the snaps at the wrist and went on wearing them, and I liked Alberto, too, and continued to see him. After twenty-six years life had seemed empty and sad because no man had ever paid any attention to me, much less given me gifts. It was all very easy for Francesca to talk that way, when she had everything she wanted and was always travelling and amusing herself.

Then summer came and I went to Maona. I expected Alberto to write, but he never sent me anything but his signature on a picture postcard of a village on the lakes. I was bored with Maona and the days seemed never to go by. I sat in the kitchen or stretched out on my bed to read. My mother, with her head wrapped in a napkin, peeled tomatoes on the porch and laid them out to dry on a board, for making preserves, while my father sat on the wall of the square in front of our house with the vet and the tax collector, tracing signs in the dust with his cane. The maidservant washed clothes at the fountain in the courtyard and wrung them out with her heavy red arms; flies buzzed over the tomatoes, and my mother wiped her knife on a newspaper and dried her sticky hands. I looked at Alberto's postcard until I knew the contents of the picture by heart: a ray of sun striking a sailing boat on the lake. Why had he sent me nothing but this?

Francesca wrote me two letters from Rome, where she had gone with a friend to study at a school of dramatics. First she said that she was engaged to be married and then that it was all off.

I often thought that Alberto might come to Maona to see me. My father would be surprised until I explained that he was a friend of Dr. Gaudenzi. I used to go into the kitchen and carry the garbage pail down to the coal cellar because it had such a bad smell, but the maidservant said that it had no smell at all and carried it back to the kitchen. On the one hand I was afraid to see Alberto appear, because I was ashamed of the garbage pail and of the way my mother looked with a napkin wrapped around her head and her hands sticky with tomatoes; on the other, I waited eagerly for his arrival, and every time the bus came I looked out the window to see if he was on it. I breathed hard and shook all over every time I saw a slight figure in a light raincoat get off, but when I realized that it was not Alberto I went back into my room to read and day-dream until dinner. Often I tried to dream again of the man with the broad shoulders and ironical manner, but he drifted farther and farther away until his anonymous and changing face lost all significance.

When I came back to the city I expected that Alberto would turn up soon. He must guess that I had to return for the opening of school. Every evening I powdered and primped and sat waiting; then, when he failed to come, I went to bed. The boarding-house was gloomy and desolate with its dark flowered hangings and upholstery and the screeching of the landlady's daughter when she refused to get undressed. I had Alberto's address and telephone number, but I didn't dare try to get in touch with him because he had always taken the initiative of telephoning me. Perhaps, I thought, he had not yet come back. One day I called his number from a public telephone booth and his voice answered. But I hung up the receiver without saying a word. Every evening I primped and powdered and waited. I was half ashamed of myself and tried to cover up my air of expectancy by reading a book, but the words made no sense. The nights were still warm, and through the open window I could hear the trams on the boulevards. I imagined him riding in one of them with his light raincoat and leather brief-case, going about one of the mysterious activities which he was never willing to talk about.

This, then, is how I fell in love with him, sitting all powdered and primped in my boarding-house bedroom while the half-hours and hours went by, accompanied by the screeching of the landlady's daughter, or walking in the city streets, on the alert for his unexpected appearance, and with a quickened pulse every time I saw a slight figure in a light raincoat holding one shoulder a little higher than the other. I began to think constantly of his life, how he managed being in the house with a mother who studied Sanskrit and refused to put on her shoes. I said to myself that if he asked me I would marry him, and then I would know at every hour of the day where he was and what he was doing. Every evening when he came home he would throw his raincoat over a chair in the hall and I would hang it up in the closet. Francesca had not yet come back from Rome, but when she came she would surely ask about Alberto, and when I told her I had not seen him again she would exclaim: 'How does that happen, if he was in love with you?' and I would be embarrassed.

I went to the Gaudenzi house one day to see if he was there or if they had news of him. The doctor wasn't at home and his wife was washing the windows. While I watched her polish them she told me that the system was to clean them with a solution of ashes and then to rub them slowly with a wool cloth. Then she came down from the ladder and made me a cup of hot chocolate. But she said not a word about Alberto, so I went away.

Finally one day I met him on the street. I saw him from a distance with his brief-case under his arm and his raincoat open and flapping. I walked behind him for a while as he smoked a cigarette and flicked the ashes away. Then he stopped and turned around in order to stamp out the butt and saw me. He was very pleased and took me to a café. He told me that it was only because he was very busy that he had not come to call, but that he had thought of me often. I looked at him and tried to recognize in this little man with the curly black hair the cause of all my anguish and torment. I felt cold and humiliated and as if something inside me were broken. Alberto asked me how I had spent the summer and whether I had hidden in the coal cellar, and with that we both laughed. He remembered everything, without exception, that I had ever told him about myself. Then I asked him about his holiday. He immediately put on a weary and faraway expression and said that he had done nothing but look at the lake. He liked lakes, he said, because their water does not have the same violent colours and glaring light as that of the sea.

After we had sat for a short time in the café everything was just the way it had been before, and we laughed together at the stories I told him. He seemed very, very happy to be with me and I was happy too. I forgot how long a time I had waited for him in vain and told myself that if he had not been so busy he would surely have come to see me. I talked to him about my mother and father and the tax collector and the new arrivals at the boarding-house. He made a sketch of me in his notebook while I was talking, then tore it up and made another. After that he sketched the lake where he had been staying, with himself rowing a boat and old ladies standing on the shore with little wiry-haired dogs holding their tails straight up in the air while they urinated against a tree.

We started to see each other once again almost every afternoon or evening. When I went upstairs to my room I asked

myself if we were in love, without finding any answer. He
never spoke of love and neither did I. I spoke only of my
school and the boarding-house and the books I had been
reading. I thought of Alberto's slender hands sketching in
his notebook, the curly black hair around his thin face, and
his slight body in a light raincoat going about the city. I
thought about them all day long, to the exclusion of everything else: first the hands, then the notebook, then the raincoat, and then again the notebook and the curly hair showing
below his hat and the thin face and the hands. I read
Xenophon to eighteen girls in a classroom newly re-
painted in green and decorated with a map of Asia and a
portrait of the Pope; ate my meals in the boarding-house
dining-room while the landlady paced up and down among the
tables; took the bus to Maona every Saturday and felt more
and more like an idiot because I had no interest in anyone or
anything. I was no longer so sure that he loved me, although
he went on bringing me books and chocolates and seemed to
enjoy my company. But he said nothing about himself, and
while I read Xenophon to my class or put the girls' marks
down in my records, I could imagine only his slight figure
going about its mysterious activities, wrapped in a flapping
raincoat, following impulses and desires of which I was
entirely ignorant. Then something like a fever would come
over me. Once I had been a fairly good teacher and taken
considerable interest in my pupils and their work. But now I
felt not the least bit of affection for the eighteen girls in front
of me; in fact, they bored me to the point of nausea and I could
not even bear to look at them.

Francesca had come back from Rome in a very bad
humour. I went to her house for dinner one night, meaning
to leave early because Alberto might come to the boarding-
house to see me. It was an endless meal, with my aunt and
uncle having a quarrel and Francesca sitting stubbornly
silent in a stunning knitted black dress which made her look

older than usual and very pale. After dinner my aunt took me up to her room and asked me what was the matter with Francesca. I told her that I didn't know, and all the time I was impatient to go away, but she clutched my hand and cried. She said that she couldn't understand Francesca at all, especially since Francesca had begun to wear nothing but black, with black hats that made her look so much older. She couldn't make out what Francesca had been up to at the school of dramatics or what she intended to do with herself next. Francesca had got herself engaged during the summer to a promising young man of good family, but then she had thrown him over. I felt the minutes passing by and feared that Alberto might be at the boarding-house already, and here my aunt clutched my hand in hers and sniffled into her handkerchief.

It was late when I finally escaped. When I arrived at the boarding-house they were locking the doors and the maid told me that the usual gentleman had come to see me, waited for a while in the drawing-room, and then gone away. I went up to my room, got into bed, and cried. It was the first time in my life that I had cried over a man, and it seemed to me this must be a sign that I loved him. I thought how, if he asked me to marry him, I would say yes, and then we would always be together and even when he was out I would know where he was. But when I imagined our making love together I felt something like disgust and said to myself that I couldn't be in love with him after all. It was all very confusing.

But he never asked me to marry him, and we went on talking together like two good friends. He refused to speak of himself and always wanted me to do the talking. On days when I was in low spirits he seemed to be bored and I was afraid that he would never come to see me again. I forced myself to be gay and told him stories about the people at the boarding-house and the landlady's screeching daughter, which we laughed at together. But when he went away I felt tired. I stretched out on my bed and thought back to all the things I used to imagine. Now I had become too idiotic to have any imagination. I absorbed his every word and tried to see if there was any love in it. I took his words and turned them over and over again in my mind. They seemed to have first one meaning and then another, until finally I let the whole thing go and dozed off.

Once Alberto told me that he had never done anything in earnest. He knew how to draw, but he was not a painter; he played the piano without playing it well; he was a lawyer but he did not have to work for a living and it didn't make much difference whether he turned up at his office or not. For this reason he stayed in bed all morning, reading. But often he had a feeling half of shame and half of satiety and thought he was going to stifle in his soft warm bed, with its yellow silk comforter. He said that he was like a cork bobbing on the surface of the sea, pleasantly cradled by the waves but unable to know what there was at the bottom. This was all he ever said about himself, except for the fact that he liked the country around the lakes. I absorbed these words and turned them over and over in my mind, but they amounted to very little beside the great stretches of mystery in his life, where only an old lady intent on her Sanskrit and a yellow silk comforter bobbed vaguely on the waves of my imagination.

While I was sitting there in the park it began to rain. I got up, went back to the café, and sat down at a small table near a window. Peering through the glass, I suddenly began to wonder whether anyone had heard my revolver shot. Our house is at the end of a quiet street, surrounded by a garden with trees. Quite possibly no one had heard it at all. This is the house of the old lady who studied Sanskrit; the bookcases are still full of Sanskrit tomes and the old lady's odour lingers on. I never saw the old lady for myself because she died before we were married, but I saw her ivory cigarette holder lying in a box, her bedroom slippers, her crocheted wool shawl, and her powder box, empty except for a wad of cotton. And everywhere there was her odour.

When Alberto's mother died he was a wreck. He found her one morning dead in her bed. That afternoon he was to take me to an art exhibition. Finally, when he didn't turn up, I phoned him and he told me that his mother was dead. I couldn't find much to say over the telephone, so I sat down and wrote him a letter. Sometimes I can manage such things fairly well, and this one came to me easily. I didn't go to the funeral because the old lady had left the express wish that no one should be invited, at least so Dr. Gaudenzi told me when I phoned him up to inquire.

A few days later I got a note from Alberto saying that he didn't feel like going out and would I come to his house to see him. My heart beat fast at the prospect. I found Alberto unshaven and with rumpled hair, wearing a pyjama jacket over his trousers. He tried to light the stove but only managed to stuff it with newspapers without getting it to burn. I succeeded in lighting it, and we sat down close by. He showed me a picture of his mother when she was young, a large, haughty woman with a big Spanish comb stuck in her hair. He spoke of her at great length, and I could not reconcile his description of her as a kindly and sensitive soul with either the young woman in the picture or the cantankerous old lady in bedroom slippers whom I had always imagined. I looked at the stove and the room and the garden outside with its high trees and the grapevine growing on the wall. Sitting with him there in his house, I felt quieter and more peaceful than I had felt for a long time, as if the feverishness and tension of the past few months had subsided.

I was so happy when I went away that I couldn't bear to stay alone in the boarding-house and I went to see Francesca. But Francesca was in an abominable humour. She no sooner saw me than she complained of a headache and said she had no desire to listen to anyone's confidences. She lay there on her bed with a hot-water bottle and asked me to mend the lining of her coat because she had to go out. I mended it and went away.

Alberto didn't ask me to come to his house again. We went back to walking along the river and sitting for hours in cafés. Of his mother he spoke no more. He wore a black band on his coat sleeve, but he was making sketches in his note-book, including one of the two of us lighting the stove. When he went away I was left with a feeling of emptiness and stupor. For the life of me I couldn't make him out. I couldn't understand why he chose to spend so many hours with me, asking questions about the people in the boarding-house and making sketches. Not a single word of love had ever passed between us. We went for long walks along the river or in the outskirts of the city, where lovers go, and yet we exchanged none of the words or gestures of love.

So it was that I finally spoke up and said that I loved him. I was weary of the burden of my secret; often in my boarding-house room I could feel it growing within me until I thought I should burst, and all the time I was becoming more and more of an idiot, unable to take an interest in anyone or anything else. I had to find out whether he loved me, too, and whether one day we should be married. Knowing this was a necessity like eating and drinking, and all of a sudden it came to me that telling the truth was a necessity, too, no matter how difficult it seemed. And so I said that I loved him.

We were leaning up against the wall of a bridge. It was dark and wagons were passing slowly along the street with paper lanterns swinging under the horses' bellies, while birds whirred out of the tall rough grass beside the river. We had stood there silently for some minutes, watching darkness fall and the lights come on in the last scattered houses of the city. Alberto was telling me how as a little boy he had loved those paper lanterns and waited every year for the holiday when they were strung up on every balcony, only to be torn down, in melancholy fashion, the morning after. Then it was that I came out with the whole thing. I told him how I tormented myself waiting for him at the boarding-house, how I couldn't concentrate on correcting my school papers, how I was gradually turning into a complete idiot, all because I loved him. I turned to look at him after I had spoken, and on his face there was a sad and frightened expression, which I knew meant he didn't love me at all. I began to cry and he pulled out a handkerchief to dry my tears. He was pale and frightened and said that he had never dreamed such a thing could happen. He enjoyed my company and considered me a good friend, but he simply didn't care for me that way. He said there was a woman he had been in love with for years. He couldn't marry her because she was already married, but he didn't think he could ever live with anyone else. He had made a great mistake to hurt me, but quite unintentionally, without ever dreaming that it could be so serious.

We went back to the city without speaking. When we said good-night at the boarding-house door he asked if he could come back the next day and I said I preferred never to see him again. 'All right,' he said as he started to go. I watched him walk away looking somehow humiliated, with the bent shoulders and slow, tired steps of a boy who has taken a beating.

I went up to bed without any dinner, leaving word with the maid to call Francesca and ask her if she could come over. Francesca had freshly plucked eyebrows and looked very handsome in her black knitted dress and a turban with a silk pendant. She sat on the edge of my bed, lit a cigarette, and said:

'Out with it!' But I could not speak through my tears, so she smoked and waited for me to pull myself together. 'Still the same old guy?' she asked.

'Yes,' I answered. She grimaced and blew out a mouthful of smoke.

'I simply can't see him,' she said.

Little by little I told her the whole story. She stayed until midnight and we had to call the maid to open the front door and let her out. Francesca left me some sleeping pills, but I couldn't close my eyes all night long. Every now and then, as I began to doze off, Alberto's sad and frightened face surged up before me. I asked myself what I was going to do with my life and felt ashamed of the way I had spoken. Every word either one of us had said there on the bridge came back to haunt me.

Francesca returned the next morning and brought me some oranges. She sent the maid to the school to say that I had bronchitis and wrote a letter to my mother telling her that I wouldn't be home for the week-end because I was under the weather. She peeled an orange for me, but I couldn't eat it, so she ate it herself and told me to spend the day in bed. The only thing to do, she said, was to go and stay for two months with her at San Remo. I said I couldn't move on account of the school, and besides I hadn't the money. 'Who gives a rap for that filthy school?' she said, and added that she had plenty of money for both of us and that we were leaving the very next day. When we got to San Remo she would lend me her low-necked pink tulle dress with the two blue roses on one shoulder. She pulled my suitcase out of the cupboard, wiped it off with a newspaper, and began to pack my clothes, then she went home to have lunch and do her own packing.

I stayed in bed for a while, thinking about the woman Alberto loved. I could see her standing motionless in front of me, staring at me out of cruel, stupid eyes that were set in a wide, heavily powdered face. She had a soft and abundantly curving figure and slender hands loaded with rings. Then this image faded away and I saw her as a weary hag with an outmoded wide-brimmed hat and a lean and hungry look about her. The weary hag was sorry for me, but I couldn't bear her presence in the room, and her compassionate expression froze me with horror. I asked myself what I was going to do with my life, and all the words exchanged between Alberto and myself flowed to and fro somewhere inside of me. My mouth was bitter and dry and my head throbbed.

The maid came up to tell me that the usual gentleman was downstairs in the drawing-room. I got up, dressed, and went down. Alberto was sitting there with his brief-case on his knees and the shivery, cowed appearance of a little boy who had just had a caning. He said he hadn't been able to sleep, and I said I hadn't either. We went out to a café together and sat at the far end of a dark, deserted room decorated with mirrors that had *Cinzano Vermouth* painted in red letters across them. They were playing billiards next door, and we could hear the knocking of balls and the hum of voices. Alberto said he couldn't get along without seeing me and that he had spent a very bad night thinking about how much he had hurt me. Since his mother had died the house was very lonely and the days when he didn't see me were empty and cold. I reminded him of the other woman. But he said she was often unkind to him and his life was entirely without joy. He felt stupid and useless, like a cork bobbing on the water.

I didn't go to San Remo. When Francesca came back I told her I didn't want to go. She lost her temper, threw the oranges on the floor, and kicked my suitcase over. The colonel's widow began to knock on the wall with her hairbrush. I told Francesca that San Remo was the last place in the world I wanted to go to, that I hated the violent colours and glaring light of the sea. I said I'd rather give up the ghost in my own room in the boarding-house than board a train and go away. If you're in trouble, I told her, it's better to stew in your own juice in familiar surroundings. A change of air is positively fatal.

'Look out for yourself, then,' she said. 'And next time you're on your deathbed don't call me. I've better things to do.' She jammed her turban on her head and looked at herself in the mirror while she buttoned up her coat and smoothed it over her hips.

When Alberto asked me to marry him I said yes. I asked him how he expected to live with me if he was in love with somebody else, and he said that if I loved him very much and was very brave we might make out very well together. Plenty of marriages are like that, he said, because it's very unusual for both partners to love each other the same way. I wanted to know a lot more about his feelings for me, but I couldn't talk to him for long about anything important because it bored him to try to get to the bottom of things and turn them over and over the way I did. When I began to speak of the woman he loved and to ask if he still went to see her, his eyes dimmed and his voice became tired and faraway and he said that she was a bad woman, that she had caused him a great deal of pain and he didn't want to be reminded of her.

So he said that we'd get married and we went on seeing each other. Now he held my hands and kissed me when we were alone in a café or beside the river, but he never set any definite month or day for our wedding. Finally I told him that we must go together to Maona and he must speak to my father about it. He didn't seem very enthusiastic, but he came. I wrote to my mother to take the garbage pail out of the kitchen and cook a good dinner for Saturday night because I was bringing someone with me.

We took the usual bus and Alberto made sketches of all the people on it. When we got to Maona my mother and father were somewhat taken aback, but Alberto reassured them by asking to speak to my father alone. They went into the smaller parlour together and my mother took in a brazier of coals to warm it up. Afterward my father came out looking very happy and we all drank marsala together. But my mother took me aside and half cried. Alberto seemed so old, she said, and then he only came up to my shoulder, whereas in her opinion a man ought to be taller than his wife. She asked me if I was sure I loved him, and when I said yes she took me up to her room to show me the bed and table linen she had set aside for the day of my marriage. Alberto spent the whole day chatting in the kitchen. My mother had taken the garbage pail away and bought two salt cellars so that the salt should not come to the table in a saucer. The vet and the tax collector dropped in after supper, and Father introduced Alberto as my fiancé. Alberto played a game of chess with the tax collector and then we drank some more marsala. Alberto became great friends with the tax collector, and before going back to the city that evening he promised to send him some Danish stamps for his collection.

Later that night, in my own room, when I was getting· undressed and going to bed in the bed I had slept in ever since I was a child, a wave of terror and disgust came over me at the thought that soon Alberto and I would be married and make love together. I reassured myself with the idea that this was only because I had never made love before, but I remembered the slight disgust I felt every time he kissed me and wondered whether or not I really loved him. It's very difficult, I thought to myself, to know what we're really like inside. When it had seemed as if he were going out of my life I had felt so sad that I didn't want to go on living, and yet when he entered my life as he did just now when he talked to my father and mother I was filled with terror and disgust. But I came to the conclusion that I only needed to be a little braver because all girls must feel somewhat the same way. It's probably a mistake to follow every meandering of our feelings and waste time listening to every echo from within. That, in fact, is no way to live.

I stayed at Maona all day Sunday while my father went to

the city to see Dr. Gaudenzi and find out something more about Alberto. He seemed quite pleased when he came back in the evening and said that he was glad I had found the proper sort of man and one of good social standing. My mother cried and said that marriage was a lottery, but he told her that she was being very silly and that women always have some excuse for shedding a few tears.

Before we were married, when we went for a walk or sat in a café, Alberto enjoyed my company even if he wasn't in love with me. He went out of his way to call on me; yes, even if it was raining he never failed to come. He sketched my face in his notebook and listened to what I had to say.

But after we were married he didn't sketch my face any more. He drew animals and trains, and when I asked him whether trains meant that he wanted to go away he only laughed and said no. He did go away, though, after we had been married just a month, and didn't turn up for ten days. One morning I found him packing his bag and he said he was going to the country with Augusto to revisit some of the scenes of their youth. He didn't ask me if I wanted to go; in fact, such a thought had apparently not even occurred to him. But this didn't particularly surprise me. Augusto and he had been boys together, and their friendship was so close that they had a way of talking to each other in something like a code which no outsider could decipher. And then he had said once that Augusto didn't like me. I wasn't too badly hurt, but I decided it was up to me to make myself agreeable to Augusto so that the next time they went anywhere together they'd ask me to come along. I, too, liked to wander about the countryside, but perhaps he didn't know it.

We had a sixteen-year-old girl called Gemma for a maid, the daughter of the shoemaker at Maona. She was very silly and had an unpleasant way of laughing through her nose. She had a notion that there were mice in the house, although I never saw any myself, and she used to sleep with her head under the covers for fear the mice would jump on her bed and eat her up. Finally she came back from Maona one day with a cat and talked to him while she did the cleaning. The cat used to run into the room where the old lady had died, and Gemma was afraid to go after him because she had a peasant belief that the old lady would pop out of a closet and strike her blind. The cat would sit purring on an armchair and Gemma would stand in the doorway trying to lure him out with scraps of cheese. I used to go into this room frequently myself, because I liked to picture the old lady in my imagination and catch the odour of her that lingered in the empty powder box and the tasselled curtains. Her armchair and footstool still stood beside the window, and her black dress and crocheted shawl were hanging in the closet.

Alberto's study was locked. Every time he went out of the house he locked the door and put the key in his pocket. When I asked him why, he said because there was a loaded revolver in the drawer of the desk. There was no lock on the drawer, so he locked the door of the room instead. With that he laughed and said he didn't want to put ideas in my head. For years and years he'd kept that revolver loaded in case he ever wanted to kill somebody, or perhaps commit suicide. Keeping it that way was such a habit that he was almost superstitious about it. He said Augusto kept a loaded revolver in the drawer of his desk too.

While Alberto was away I often stopped in front of that door. It wasn't on account of the revolver, I told myself, that he kept it locked. Perhaps there were letters and pictures in his desk. I was sorry that I hadn't anything to hide from him, that he knew everything there was to know about me. Before I met him my life had been colourless and dull. And after our marriage I had let everything go. I had stopped teaching and saw Francesca very infrequently. Ever since she had offered to take me to San Remo and I had let her down she had shown little desire to see me. I felt that she was making an effort not to say anything disagreeable and looked back sentimentally to the time when she used to bully and scold me instead of being distant and polite. The Gaudenzis used to ask Alberto and me to their house in the evening. They were always very nice and said they felt they had a share in our happiness because it was through them that we had met. But Alberto said they were stupid and uninteresting and he was always finding excuses to stay away. What he did like, however, was to have Augusto drop in. They would sit and talk in the study and I went to bed, because Alberto said that it embarrassed Augusto to see me.

A few days after Alberto had gone I met Augusto in the street. He was walking along with his overcoat collar turned up and his hands in his pockets, and he looked at me hard out of his strong stony face. I began to shake so that I couldn't say a word, and he nodded to me and walked hurriedly on. So now I knew that Alberto had lied when he told me he was going away with Augusto. I went back to the house and sat down by the stove and the cat crept up into my lap. Then it was that I thought for the first time that our marriage was a big mistake. I sat there stroking the cat and staring through the window at the leaves on the trees, which had turned pink in the glow of the sunset. All of a sudden I realized that I felt like a guest in this house. I never thought of it as mine, or the garden either, and I felt guilty whenever Gemma broke a plate, even if Alberto didn't say anything. Sometimes I half imagined that the old lady actually would pop out of a closet and chase Gemma and the cat and myself away. But where, then, could I feel at home? In my room at Maona my mother had begun to store potatoes and jars of tomato preserve. For a moment I wished I were back in the boarding-house, with the landlady's hysterical daughter and the flowered hangings, boiling an egg over an alcohol flame.

Finally I had supper and went to bed. But it was cold and I

lay there with my teeth chattering instead of going to sleep.
Here in this bed we had made love for the first time when we
came back from our fortnight's honeymoon on the lakes. I
was disgusted and ashamed every time Alberto made love to
me, but I imagined that all women must feel the same way at
the start. I liked best to lie quietly and feel him sleeping
beside me. I told him the way I felt about making love and
asked him if other women felt the same way. He answered
that he didn't know how the devil it was with women. The
main thing for a woman was to have a baby, and for a man
too. And I ought to cure myself of the habit of thinking about
things so hard.

It had never occurred to me that he could lie. I had helped
him pack his bag and made him take a blanket with him
because I thought he might be cold in the inns and farm-
houses where he said he would stay. He didn't want to take
it, but I insisted. Then he left the house in a great hurry, saying that Augusto was waiting for him at the station.

I thought of our love-making and the tender, feverish
words he whispered in my ear. Then he would fall asleep and
I could hear his steady breathing beside me. I would lie awake
in the darkness and try to remember every word he had said.
I didn't care much for the love-making, but I enjoyed lying
awake in the darkness and saying his words over and over to
myself.

He hadn't gone away with Augusto, then. He had gone
with that woman. Doubtless this wasn't the first time he
had lied to me; doubtless they had gone on meeting
even after he had decided to marry. When he said he was
going to the office, perhaps he was going to see her instead.
They were making love together and he said the same
feverish words to her as he said to me. Then he probably lay
quietly at her side and they sighed over the fact that they
must live apart. I could see the woman standing motionless in
the darkness before me, wearing a shiny silk dress and

quantities of jewels. She yawned and pulled down her stockings with an indolent gesture. Then she disappeared, only to
turn up again in a tall and masculine guise, striding along with
a Pekinese dog in her arms.

Alberto stayed away ten days. The evening he came back
he seemed tired and in a bad humour and he asked for a cup of
very hot coffee. Gemma had already gone to bed, so I made
the coffee and took it to him in our room. He drank it very
slowly, staring at me all the while but making no motion to
kiss me.

'You weren't with Augusto,' I said. 'Who were you with?'

He put the cup on the table, got up, and scratched his head.
Then he took off his jacket and tie and threw them on the
chair.

'I'm sleepy and tired,' he said. 'I don't feel like talking.'

'Augusto was here all the time,' I said. 'I saw him on the
street. Who were you with?'

'Alone,' he answered. 'I was alone.' We got into bed and
I put out the light. Suddenly Alberto's voice rose up out of
the darkness.

'It was anything but a pleasant trip,' he said. 'I'd have
done better to stay at home.' He edged up to me and held me
tight. 'Don't ask any questions,' he added. 'I feel worn out
and terribly sad. Just be silent and very, very still.'

'Is she as bad as all that?' I asked.

'She's unfortunate,' he said, running his hands over my
body. 'She can't help being unkind.'

Hot, silent tears streamed down my cheeks. He touched
my face with his hands and held me tighter.

'A perfectly hellish trip,' he said, and I heard him laughing
under his breath. 'Don't ask any questions. Don't ever ask
any questions. You're all I've got. Just remember that.'

His hand lay on my shoulder, and I put out my hand to
touch his thin, hot face. For the first time I wasn't disgusted
when we made love.

A few months later Alberto went away again. I didn't ask him any questions. He was packing his bag in the study and I saw him put in a volume of Rilke. He used to read Rilke's poems out loud to me, too, in the evening. When he went out the door he said:

'I'll be back in a fortnight.'

Then he turned the key in the lock, something he never forgot to do. I smiled at him as he left. The smile was still on my lips when I went back up the stairs and into my room, and I tried to keep it there as long as I could. I sat down in front of the mirror and brushed my hair, still with that silly smile on my face. I was pregnant and my face was pale and heavy. The letters I wrote to my mother had in them the same cowardly and idiotic smile. I hadn't gone to Maona for some time because I was afraid of the questions my mother might ask me.

'You're all I've got. Just remember that.' Yes, I had re-membered; indeed these words had helped me to go on living from day to day. But little by little they had lost their sweet-ness, like a prune stone that has been sucked too long. I didn't ask Alberto anything. When he came back to the house late at night I never asked him what he had been doing. But I had waited for him so long that a burden of silence had accumu-lated inside me. I looked in vain for something amusing to say to him so that he wouldn't be too bored with me. I sat knitting under the lamp while he read the paper, cleaning his teeth with a toothpick and scratching his head. Sometimes he sketched in his notebook, but he no longer drew my face. He drew trains and little horses galloping away with their tails streaming in the wind. And now that we had a cat he did cats and mice too. Once I told him that he should put my face on a mouse and his on a cat. He laughed and asked me why. So I asked him if he didn't think we two fitted into these roles. He laughed again and said there was nothing mouselike about me. Still he did draw a mouse with my face and a cat with his. The mouse was knitting, with a frightened and ashamed expression on its face, and the cat was angrily making a sketch in a notebook.

The evening after he had gone away for the second time Augusto came to see me and stayed quite late. He said that Alberto had asked him to keep me company sometimes in the evening while he was gone. I was taken aback and couldn't find anything to say. He sat there with his pipe between his teeth and an ugly grey wool scarf thrown around his neck, staring at me silently out of his square stony face with the black moustache. Finally I asked him if it was true that he didn't like me. He turned brick-red up to the eyebrows and then we had a good laugh together. That's how we started being friends. Sometimes when two people don't know what to say to each other some such trivial remark will turn the trick. Augusto told me that on general principles he didn't like anybody, that the only person he'd ever really liked was himself. Whenever he was in a bad humour, he said, he looked at himself in the mirror and began to smile and then he felt positively cheerful. I told him that I had tried smiling at myself in the mirror, too, but it didn't do any good. He asked me if I was in a bad humour very often and I said yes, I was. He stood in front of me with his pipe in his hand, blowing smoke out between his closed lips.

'That woman, Augusto . . .' I said. 'What's she like?'

'What woman?' he asked.

'The woman who goes on trips with Alberto.'

'Look here,' he said. 'It's no use talking about her. Besides, it doesn't seem right.'

'I don't know anything about her,' I said, 'not even her name. And I torment myself trying to imagine her face.'

'Her name is Giovanna,' he said. 'And her face—well, her face isn't anything special.'

'Isn't she very beautiful?' I asked.

'How should I know?' he said. 'I'm not an expert on

beauty. Yes, she's beautiful, I suppose, when you come down to it. Or at least she was when she was young.'

'Is she no longer young, then?'

'Not so very,' he said. 'But what's the point of discussing her?'

'Please,' I said. 'I'd like to be able to talk to you about her once in a while. It gets on my nerves to mope all by myself. I don't know a thing, you see. I didn't even know her name. I feel as if I were in the dark, as if I were blind and groping my way around, touching the walls and the objects in the room.' My ball of yarn fell to the floor and Augusto bent over to pick it up.

'Why the devil did you two marry?' he asked.

'Yes,' I said. 'I made a mistake. He wasn't very keen on it, but he didn't stop to think. He doesn't like to think about important things. In fact, he hates people who are always searching inside themselves and trying to find some meaning to life. When he sees me sitting still and thinking he lights a cigarette and goes away. I married him because I wanted to know all the time where he was. But the way it turned out, he knows where I am—I'm just sitting here, waiting for him to come home—and I don't know where he is any more than I did before. He isn't really my husband. A husband is a man that—well, that you always know where he is. And if someone asks you: "Where's your husband?" then you ought to be able to answer without hesitation. Whereas I don't go out of the house for fear of meeting people I know and hearing them ask: "Where is he?" Because I shouldn't know what to answer. You may think I'm very silly, but I don't go out of the house.'

'Why did you marry?' he repeated. 'What got into you?' I began to cry. 'It was a hell of an idea,' he said, blowing the smoke out of his mouth and then staring at me in silence. He had a stubborn and gloomy expression on his face, as if he refused to be sorry for me.

98

'But where's Alberto?' I asked him. 'Do you know where he is now?'

'No, I don't,' Augusto answered. 'I've got to go. Good night.' He scraped the ashes out of his pipe with a matchstick and took his coat off the chair. Now his tall and solitary figure was standing in the doorway. 'There isn't anything I can do about it,' he said. 'Good night.'

I couldn't close an eye all night long. I imagined that Augusto had fallen in love with me and I was his mistress. Every day I would go to meet him at a hotel. I would come home very late and Alberto would search my face agonizingly to see where I had been. But when Augusto came to see me again a few evenings later I was ashamed of all the things I had imagined. He picked up my ball of wool when it fell to the floor, filled his pipe, lit it, scraped the ashes out of it with a matchstick, and paced up and down the room, while all the time I imagined how we would make love in a hotel room and blushed with shame at my own imaginings. I didn't speak again of Alberto and myself and neither did he. We didn't know what to talk about, and I had an idea he was as bored as I was. Only I was glad we had become friends, and I told Alberto as much when he came back. He didn't say anything, but he didn't look very pleased. He shouted and made a great fuss in the bathroom because the water was too hot and he couldn't find his shaving brush and the other things he was looking for. He came out of the bathroom freshly shaved, with a lighted cigarette in his mouth, and I asked him if this trip had been any more of a success than the one before. He said that it was a trip like any other and not worth talking about, that he had gone on business to Rome. I said I wished he wouldn't go away again before the baby was born because I was afraid of what might happen if I had pains during the night when I was all alone. He said I wasn't the first woman in the world to have a baby and if I was so nervous it was just too bad. We didn't say anything more, but

I cried over my knitting, and then he went out, slamming the door behind him.

Augusto came to the house that evening and I kept him in the drawing-room, where Alberto told him that he'd been on a business trip to Rome and thanked him for keeping me company. A little later Gemma called me into the kitchen to look over the household accounts, and when I came back the two men had gone into the study. I wondered whether to join them there or to wait in the drawing-room, and after considerable hesitation I decided that there was nothing so strange about my going to join them. I picked up my knitting and started to go into the study, but the door was locked and I could hear Alberto saying: 'It's quite useless.' What did he mean? I sat down in the drawing-room and began to count stitches. I felt tired and heavy and the baby stirred inside of me. Then and there I wanted to die with my baby, to escape from this torment and not feel anything more. I went to bed and to sleep but woke up when Alberto came in.

'I'm not afraid any more; I only want to die,' I said.

'Go to sleep and don't be silly,' he answered. 'I don't want you to die.'

'What difference would it make to you?' I asked him. 'You have Augusto and Giovanna. You don't need me. You don't need the baby either. What will you do with a baby anyhow? You've grown old without ever having a baby and you got along perfectly well without it.'

'I'm not so old,' he said with a laugh. 'I'm only forty-four.'

'You are old, though,' I said. 'You have a lot of grey hair. You got along without a baby for forty-four years. What will you do with one now? It's too late for you to get used to having a baby crying about the house.'

'Please don't say such silly things,' he said. 'You know perfectly well I'm anxious to have this baby.'

'Why didn't you ever have one with Giovanna?'

Out of the darkness he gave a deep sigh.

'I've asked you not to talk about that person.'

I sat bolt upright in the bed.

'Don't say "that person." Say "Giovanna."'

'As you like.'

'Say "Giovanna."'

'Giovanna, then.'

'Why didn't you ever have a baby together?'

'I don't think she ever wanted to have a baby by me.'

'No? Then she can't love you very much.'

'I don't think she does love me very much.'

'I don't love you either. No one can love you. Do you know why? Because you have no courage. You're a little man who hasn't enough courage to get to the bottom of anything. You're a cork bobbing on the surface, that's what you are. You don't love anybody and nobody loves you.'

'You don't love me, then?' he asked.

'No.'

'When did you stop loving me?'

'I don't know. Some time ago.'

Once more he sighed.

'It's all too bad,' he said.

'Alberto,' I said, 'tell me where you were these last few days.'

'In Rome, on business.'

'Alone or with Giovanna?'

'Alone.'

'Do you swear it?'

'I don't want to swear,' he said.

'Because it isn't true. That's why. You were with Giovanna. Where did you go? To the lakes? Did you go to the lakes?'

He put on the light, got up, and took a blanket out of the cupboard.

'I'm going to sleep in my study. Both of us will get more rest that way.'

He stood there in the middle of the room with the blanket over his arm, a slight figure in rumpled blue pyjamas, with his hair in disorder and a look of weariness and distress in his eyes.

'No, Alberto, don't go away; I don't want you to go away.' I was weeping and trembling and he came over and stroked my hair. I took his hand and kissed it. 'It's not true that I don't love you,' I said. 'I love you more than you can possibly know. I couldn't live with any other man. I couldn't make love with Augusto or with anybody else. I like making love with you. I'm your wife. I'm always thinking of you when you're away. I can't think of anything else, no matter how hard I try. It's idiotic of me, I know, but I can't help it. I think of every single thing that's happened to us since the day we first met. I'm glad I'm your wife.'

'Then everything's all right,' he said, picking up the blanket. He went to sleep in the study, and it was a long time before we slept together again.

It was dark when I left the café. The rain had stopped, but the pavement was still glistening. I realized that I was very tired and I had a burning feeling in my knees. I walked about the city for a while longer, then I took a tram and got off in front of Francesca's house. There were bright lights in the drawing-room, and I could see a maid passing a tray. Then I remembered that it was Wednesday, and Wednesday was Francesca's day for receiving her friends at home, so I didn't go in. I went on walking. My feet were heavy and tired, and there was a hole in the heel of my left stocking, where my shoe rubbed against the bare skin and gave me pain. Sooner or later, I thought, I'd have to go home. I shivered and a wave of nausea came over me, so I went back to the park. I sat down on a bench and slipped off my shoe to look at the sore spot on the back of my heel. The heel was swollen and red; a blister had formed and broken and now it was bleeding. Couples were embracing each other on the park benches, and in the shadow of the trees an old man lay asleep under a dark green coat.

I shut my eyes and remembered certain afternoons when I used to take the baby out in the park. We used to walk very, very slowly and I would give her warm milk out of a thermos bottle I carried in my bag. I had an enormous bag where I used to put all the baby's things: a rubber bib and one of towelling and some little raisin biscuits that she especially liked, sent by my mother from Maona. Those were long afternoons I used to spend in the park, turning around to watch the baby follow me in her velvet-edged hood, her little coat with the velvet buttons, and her white leggings. Francesca had given her a camel that swayed its head as it walked. It was a lovely camel with a gold-embroidered red cloth saddle, and it swayed its head in a very wise and appealing way. Every other minute the camel would get tangled up in its string and fall and we had to set it on its feet again. Then we walked slowly on among the trees in the warm, humid sunshine. The baby's mittens would come off and I would lean over to pull them on and blow her nose and then carry her when she was tired.

I would go home for the night, I thought, and to the police station in the morning. I didn't know where the police station was, so I'd have to look it up in the telephone book. I'd ask them to let me tell the whole story, from the very first day, including certain details which might seem trivial enough but had considerable importance. It was a long story, but they'd have to let me talk. I tried to imagine the face of the man who would listen to me, and I saw him, with a moustache and an olive complexion, sitting behind a desk. I shivered again and suddenly I wanted to phone Augusto and Francesca and ask them to go to the police station for me. Or else I might write a letter to the police and wait for them to come and pick me up at home. Of course they'd put me in jail, but I couldn't exactly imagine how that would be. All I could see was the police station and a man with a long, shiny, olive-skinned face behind a desk. When he laughed it made me shiver, and then everything was a blank, days and years tumbling out of my life that had no connection with the days and years that had been filled with the baby and Alberto and Augusto and Francesca and Gemma and the cat and my father and mother at Maona. It didn't matter at this point whether or not I went to jail. Everything that mattered had happened already, for everything that mattered was Alberto at the moment when I shot him and he fell heavily across the table and I closed my eyes and ran out of the room.

Our little girl was born three years ago on January eleventh at three o'clock in the afternoon. I trailed around the house in a wrapper, moaning with pain, for two whole days while Alberto followed me with a frightened look on his face. Dr. Gaudenzi came to take care of me, bringing a young and obnoxious nurse who called Alberto 'Daddy.' The nurse had a fight with Gemma in the kitchen because she said the kettles were dirty. They needed lots of hot water, and Gemma was terrified by my moans and groans, besides having a stye in her eye that made her particularly unintelligent. My father and mother came too. I wandered about the house making senseless remarks to the effect that they must hurry up and help me to get rid of that infernal baby. Then I was so dead tired I went to bed and fell asleep for a minute, only to wake up shrieking with pain until the nurse told me I'd get a goitre from straining my throat that way. I had forgotten the baby and Alberto, and all I wanted was to go to sleep and stop suffering. I no longer wanted to die; in fact, I was scared to pieces of dying and asked nothing more than to live. I begged everyone to tell me when the pain would be over, but it lasted a very long time, while the nurse went to and fro with kettles of water, my mother huddled in her black dress in a corner, and Alberto held my hand. But I didn't want his hand; I only bit the sheet and tried, regardless of the baby, to get rid of that terrible pain in my middle.

Then the baby was born and suddenly all my pain was gone. I raised my head to look at her as she lay there naked and red between my legs, and Alberto leaned over me with relief and joy on his face while I felt happier than I had ever felt in my life, with the pain gone from my body, leaving me with a sense of glory and peace.

My mother put the baby in bed beside me, wrapped in a white shawl with her two cold, red fists and her damp, bald little head sticking out. I saw Gemma's face leaning over with a glorious smile, and my mother's face had a glorious smile on it, too, while the baby's feeble whimpering in the shawl filled me with joy.

Everyone said I ought to sleep, but now I didn't want to. I talked incessantly and asked how the baby looked and what kind of a nose and mouth and forehead she had. They closed the shutters and took the baby away, leaving Alberto alone with me, and we laughed together over the stye in Gemma's eye and the nurse's way of calling him 'Daddy.' Alberto asked me if I still wanted to die, and I told him that was the last thing I wanted to do, but I did want a glass of orange juice because I was thirsty. He went to get the juice and brought it to me on a tray, holding up my head while I drank it and planting a gentle kiss on my hair.

The baby was very ugly at first, and Alberto called her the 'little toad.' Every time he came back from outside the first thing he asked was: 'What's the little toad up to?' Then he stood with his hands in his pockets, looking down into her cradle. He even bought a camera to take pictures of her as soon as she was slightly better to look at.

My father and mother went away after a few days, and when my mother asked me at the last minute whether I was happy I told her I most certainly was. She sent me a big box of woollens for the baby and a pair of socks she had knitted for Alberto, while my father sent a case of wine. It made them happy to think that all was going well with me, and my mother wrote to me that because Alberto was thin and had no appetite I should see to it that he didn't overwork and that the baby didn't disturb his sleep.

Probably my mother thought that we would sleep together again now that the baby was born, but he went right on sleeping in the study, as he had ever since coming back from his last trip, and I kept the baby's crib near my bed. But I couldn't sleep very well because I got up frequently to see how the baby was sleeping and whether she was hot or cold and to listen to her regular breathing. After the first few months she became very bad and woke up crying all the time, until I picked her up and rocked her in my arms. I was afraid that Alberto would hear her, so I picked her up in a hurry and walked up and down the room, singing to her in a low voice. That way she got worse and worse. She liked to have me rock her and would apparently fall asleep in my arms with her eyes shut and her breathing even, but just as soon as I put her down in the crib she started crying again. As a result I was sleepy all day long.

I didn't have much milk to give her, so I stuffed myself with food until I was quite fat. But the baby stayed thin, and when I took her out in her carriage I used to look at the other babies and ask how old they were and how much they weighed and feel ashamed because mine wasn't as fat and strong as the rest. I hastened to weigh her immediately after every time I gave her the breast and every Saturday, without her clothes on, just before her bath. I kept a notebook, where I wrote down in red ink her weekly weight and in green her increase of weight after every feeding. Saturdays I got up with a pounding heart, hoping that she would be a little heavier than the week before, but often she wasn't and I was plunged into despair. Alberto got angry with me about this and said that he had been a thin baby himself. He teased me about the notebook and about the way my hands trembled when I was dressing or undressing the baby, the way I upset the talcum powder and rushed breathlessly around the howling baby. He made a sketch of me with my mouth full of safety-pins and a breathless, frightened air about me, letting the belt of my open wrapper drag on the floor, and wearing my hair in a net because I didn't feel like combing it.

I didn't let Gemma touch the baby; in fact, I was distressed whenever she went over to whisper sweet nothings in her ear and to shake her rattle with damp, red hands. I didn't even like to see Augusto come into the room because I was afraid he might bring in some germs from outside. Augusto lived with a sister who had a small child, and I feared he might be the carrier of whooping cough or measles. Moreover, I was ashamed to have Augusto tell me that his sister's child was fat and strong.

When the baby was two or three months old Alberto began to take pictures of her: in her bath, on the table, bare-headed, and with her cap on. For a while this gave him great amusement and he bought a better camera and an album with a flowered cover where he pasted in the pictures with the dates when they were taken and a phrase of comment in red ink below. But this amusement soon palled, because he was a man who tired quickly of everything. One day he said he was going to visit some friends who had a villa on one of the lakes, and I saw him pack the volume of Rilke in his bag. He locked the study door, as he never forgot to do, and after he had gone I looked at the photograph album on the drawing-room table, which had remained only half filled after he lost his interest in photography. It depressed me to see the empty black pages, with the last picture of the baby holding her rattle, and written in red ink underneath it: 'We begin to play.'

There was only one thing in life that Alberto didn't tire

of, I reflected, and that was his passion for Giovanna. Because
I was sure he had gone with her to the lake and they were
sitting on a bench beside the water reading Rilke together.
He had long ago given up reading Rilke with me in the
evening and taken to reading a book or newspaper to himself,
picking his teeth or scratching his head at intervals and never
saying a word about what he was thinking. I wondered if this
might be my fault, although I had always listened attentively
and told him I liked Rilke's poems, even when they bored me.
How had Giovanna managed to hold his interest for all these
years? Perhaps she never showed that she loved him, but
tormented and deceived him so that he had not a moment
of peace and could not possibly forget her. I went over to the
cradle and felt sorry for the baby because I was the only one
who really loved her. I picked her up and unbuttoned my
dress, and while I was nursing her I thought that when
a woman has her baby in her arms nothing else should
matter.

I began to wean the baby when she was six months old
and tried to feed her a thin porridge to which she did not
take at all. Dr. Gaudenzi was very kind about coming to see
her, but occasionally he lost his patience and said that I took
things too hard and couldn't seem to relax. There he was
quite right. Every time the baby had a touch of fever I went
into a panic and didn't know what I was doing. I took her
temperature every five minutes, looked up in a book all the
diseases that she could possibly have, stopped eating my meals
and combing my hair and couldn't sleep at night. At times like
these my temper was constantly on edge and I would shout at
Gemma as if everything were her fault. Then, when the
baby's fever went down, I returned to reason, felt sorry for
the way I had treated her, and gave her a handsome present.
For a while afterward I didn't particularly want to see the
baby. I almost loathed everything connected with her: the
rattle, the talcum powder, the diapers, and all the rest, and

only wished I could read a novel or go to the theatre with friends. But I hadn't any friends, and when I opened a book it bored me and I went back to reading about infants' diseases and diet.

One evening while I was cooking the porridge Francesca turned up at the house. She was hatless and had no make-up on her face, while a lock of hair tumbling over her forehead and the raincoat thrown over her black dress gave her a gloomy and defiant air. She told me she had quarrelled with her mother and asked me if I could put her up for the night. I told Gemma to make up the couch in the drawing-room. Francesca sat down, puffed at a cigarette, and watched me give the baby her porridge, which the baby spat out as soon as I got it in her mouth.

'I couldn't stand a baby,' said Francesca. 'If ever I had a baby I'd kill myself, for sure.'

Alberto was in his study and I went to tell him that it was Francesca and that she had come to stay with us because there was something wrong at home.

'Good,' he said. He was reading a German book on Charles V and writing notes in the margin.

I put the baby to bed. Francesca was stretched out on the drawing-room couch, smoking another cigarette and looking as if the place had always been hers. She had taken off her garters and hung them over the back of an armchair, and she flicked the ashes from her cigarette on to the rug.

'Did you know he was unfaithful to you?' she asked.

'Yes, I know that.'

'Don't you care?'

'No.'

'Why don't you leave him?' she asked. 'Let's go for a trip somewhere. He's a little rat of a man. What good is he to you?'

'I love him,' I said, 'and then there's the baby.'

'But he's deceiving you. He does it in the most blatant

sort of way. I see them together sometimes. She has a behind like a cauliflower. Nothing much to look at.'

'Her name is Giovanna,' I said.

'Leave him, I say. What good is he to you?'

'So you've seen her, have you? What's she like?'

'Well . . . She doesn't know how to dress. They walk along very slowly. I see them all the time.'

'Why did you say she has a behind like a cauliflower?'

'Because that's what it's like, that's all. It's round, I mean, and she shakes it when she walks. But what do you care?'

Francesca took all her clothes off and walked up and down the room. I locked the door.

'Are you afraid that rat will see me?' she said. 'Lend me a nightgown, will you?' I brought her a nightgown and she put it on. 'I rattle around in it,' she said. 'You've got fat.'

'I'll lose weight now that the baby's weaned.'

'I don't want any children,' she said. 'I don't want to get married. Do you know why I fell out with my mother? Because there was a man they wanted me to marry. He works for a shipping company. They've been trying for ages to marry me off. But I've had enough. I'm not going home. I'll take a room somewhere and look for a job. I've had enough of family. I don't want to be tied to a husband, either. Just to get myself let down the way you are? Not me! I like going to bed with a man. But I'm all for variety. A couple of times with one man is enough for me.'

I listened to her with astonishment.

'You've had lovers, then?' I asked.

'Of course I have,' she said, laughing. 'Are you shocked?'

'No,' I said, 'but I don't understand how you can do it.'

'Do what?'

'Change all the time.'

'You don't understand?'

'No.'

'Oh, I've had a lot of men,' she said. 'First, one in Rome, when I was trying to get on the stage. I broke that off when he asked me to marry him. I was tired of him, anyhow; quite ready to throw him out of the window. But I still took such things seriously. "What kind of a girl am I?" I said to myself. "I must be a bitch if I like to change so often." Words have a way of scaring us when we're young. I still thought I ought to marry and be like everyone else. Then little by little I learned to make life less of a tragedy. We have to accept ourselves for what we are.'

'And other people for what they are, too,' I said. 'That's why I have to put up with Alberto. And then I shouldn't like to change.'

She burst out laughing and kissed me.

'Am I a bitch?' she asked.

'No, you're not a bitch,' I said. 'But you'll be alone in your old age.'

'What the devil do I care about that? I'll kill myself when I'm forty. Or else you'll walk out on this little rat and we'll live together.'

I kissed her and went into my room. My head was whirling with a medley of words: rat, cauliflower, bitch, accepting people for what they are, and killing oneself. I could see Alberto walking slowly along with Giovanna the way he used to walk with me before we were married. Now we never went for a walk together at all. Finally I went to bed. I had a strong urge to go into the study and stretch out beside him in his bed. I wanted to put my head on his shoulder and ask him why we never went for any more walks. I wanted to tell him that I could never change to another man. But I was afraid he might think I was there just in order to make love with him, so I stayed in my own bed, waiting for sleep to come.

Francesca stayed with us three weeks. I was very happy all this time, and it did me good to talk to her. I was no longer

so nervous over the baby's diarrhoea, and when I did show
some nervousness she teased me out of it. Sometimes she
persuaded me to leave the baby with Gemma while we went
to a moving picture together. It was fun to get up in the
morning, find Francesca wandering about the house in a long
white satin wrapper and cold cream on her face, and pass the
time of day with her until it was time for lunch. It was, in
fact, a relief to have her to talk to. I realized then how little
Alberto and I had to say to each other any more and how I
practically never felt that I could tell him what I was thinking. When he was at home he spent most of his time in the
study, which was in a state of complete disorder because he
wouldn't let anyone tidy it up. Gemma made his bed and
swept, under his strict supervision, but that was all she was
allowed to do. He forbade her to touch either his desk or
books, with the result that everything was covered with dust
and the place gave out a bad smell.

On his desk Alberto kept a picture of his mother and a
plaster bust of Napoleon that he had modelled himself when
he was sixteen years old. It looked very little like Napoleon,
but it was a good technical job. Then he had a fleet of
miniature ships which he had built as a little boy, copies
exact down to every last detail. Of these he was very
proud, particularly of a tiny sailing-boat with a pennant flying
from the mast. He asked Francesca into his study to admire
them and insisted that she examine the sailing-boat carefully.
Then he showed her his library and read some of Rilke's
poems out loud. With Francesca he was very agreeable and
in fact put himself out to please her as he always did when he
came up against somebody new. And then I fancied that
Francesca somewhat frightened him. It even occurred to me
that Giovanna tyrannized him by fright too. I was the only
person he wasn't afraid of, and perhaps that was the root of
the whole trouble. No, he certainly wasn't afraid of me.

Francesca sent me to her house for some clothes. My aunt

was there and burst into tears as soon as she saw me. She asked me any number of questions, which I didn't know how to answer. She couldn't understand why Francesca wouldn't consider the man from the shipping company, who was handsome and very much of a gentleman as well. She had never understood what Francesca wanted to do with her life, or anything else about her.

'It's this younger generation,' she said, weeping and rubbing her face with her wet handkerchief. I tried to tell her that Francesca was still young and had plenty of time ahead of her in which to find a man more to her liking. Then she told me that she didn't care for the way Francesca behaved with men, flirting with them and keeping three or four on her string at a time. I don't think for a moment that it ever remotely occurred to her that Francesca had any lovers. She did her best to understand, but the task was quite beyond her. I thought how all of us are always trying to imagine what someone else is doing, eating our hearts out trying to find the truth and moving about in our own private worlds like a blind man who gropes for the walls and the various objects in a room. Then I wrapped up Francesca's clothes and went away.

Francesca was plucking her eyebrows in the kitchen, looking into a mirror which she held in one hand. Gemma stood there gaping at her until Francesca grimaced and said:

'Run me a bath, will you, my girl?'

Gemma hurried away, laughing, and Francesca pulled her clothes out of the bundle and scrutinized them carefully, turning them over and over in her hands. I asked her whether she was ever going home.

'No,' she said dryly. 'Don't ask me again.'

I was preparing to give the baby her first orange juice and feeling a little sentimental about it. I was glad that she was turning into a big girl and starting to eat grown-up food.

'What a lot of fuss,' said Francesca as she saw me boiling a spoon. 'And when she's older she'll just be a pain in the neck the way I am to my mother. Families are a stupid invention. No marriage for me, thank you!'

I was almost jealous of Francesca. Alberto was always making up to her and sketching her face. She treated him with scorn, but when he began to make sketches of her in his notebook she came down from her high horse. In the evening Alberto would call us into his study to hear Rilke's poems and Augusto would come to join us. I decided that they might make a good match, but when I said as much to Francesca she replied that Augusto looked like a justice of the peace with his heavy moustache and scarf and the shirt sleeves that stuck out below those of his jacket. Even the man from the shipping company was a cut above him. But every time Augusto came she powdered her nose and debated in front of the mirror as to whether she should wear her best necklace.

Finally Francesca sold some of her jewels and rented a one-room apartment. She said she was going to look for a job, but meanwhile she did nothing in particular except try her hand at painting, because she claimed to have lost interest in the stage. She painted strange pictures with great splotches of colour and everything in them but the kitchen stove: houses, skulls, knights in armour, and invariably the moon. She wore a long grey linen smock and painted all day long and said that she didn't have a lover.

I was still very busy with the baby. She was just starting to walk and I had to trail her all over the house to make sure she didn't fall. She cried every time I left her alone, and I had to take her with me, even into the bathroom. She was given to tantrums and never wanted to eat her meals. I had to play with her at mealtime and get the food down without her knowing it. She staggered around the room, from chair to chair, playing with the cat and my sewing basket, and I followed her with a bowl in my hand, waiting for the right moment to slip a spoon into her mouth.

Until she was a year old the baby had lead-grey eyes, but then I noticed flecks of brown coming into them. She had very fine blonde hair which I combed back and tied with a ribbon. She was still thin and pale and not what you could call beautiful; her eyes were dull and often had dark circles around them. Eating and sleeping simply did not interest her. She cried every evening before going to sleep, and I had to walk up and down the room singing lullabies. She always wanted to hear the same thing, a French song I had learned from my mother:

> 'Le bon roi Dagobert
> A mis sa culotte à l'envers!
> Le bon Saint-Elouas
> Lui dit: O mon roi,
> Votre Majesté
> Est mal culotté.'

I used to tie a red cloth around the lamp and sing as I paced up and down with the baby in my arms. When I left the room I felt exhausted, as if from a battle. Very often I had no sooner gone out than her feeble and plaintive cry followed me and I had to go back and start all over again. She couldn't stand Alberto and cried whenever he picked her up, and he in his turn said that I had spoiled her and made her into a perfect little pest. Alberto was seldom at home and went on a number of his usual trips. When he was at home he shut himself up in the study with Augusto. But at this point I didn't particularly care what they were talking about, whether it was Giovanna or something quite different. All that mattered to me was to see the baby eat her supper until the picture of a chick emerging from the egg at the bottom of her bowl was uncovered and the bowl was empty. I remembered Alberto's telling me that a baby was the main thing in a woman's life and in a man's too. This was all very true for a woman, I reflected, but not for a man. Alberto's habits had not changed an iota since our baby was born. He took the same trips, made the same sketches in his notebook, went on jotting down phrases on the margins of his books, and continued to walk down the street at the same brisk pace as before, with a cigarette stuck between his lips. He was never upset if the baby was pale or hadn't eaten her supper. He didn't really know what she was supposed to eat, and perhaps he had not even noticed that her eyes were changing colour.

I thought I was cured of my jealousy and that I didn't care to know whether he was seeing Giovanna or not. I had borne his child and that was enough. The days when I had waited for him in the boarding-house and trembled at the mere thought of his coming now seemed so remote that I could hardly believe they belonged to the same existence. Occasionally he called me into the study to make love, but I was always on the alert for the baby's cry and didn't stop to wonder how much I enjoyed it. He didn't ask me, either, and I came to the conclusion that our marriage was no better and no worse than the run-of-the-mill variety.

One day I went for a walk with the baby. Francesca had given her the camel, and this was the first time we were taking it out. The camel was handsome and swayed its head in such a way that people stopped to look at it. We went slowly in the warm sunshine, and I was very cheerful because the baby had drunk her milk and eaten two ladyfingers. The camel kept falling down and I would stoop to pick it up and dust its red cloth saddle.

Then I saw Alberto crossing the street with a woman. All that I could see of her was that she was tall and wore a mouton fur piece. I picked the baby and the camel up in my arms and hurried back home. The baby struggled and cried because she wanted to walk, but I held her tight until I came to the door. Then I told Gemma to take off her coat and keep her in the kitchen while I wrote a letter. I shut the drawing-room door and sat down on the sofa. I had thought of Giovanna so often and pictured her as having a wide, immobile face that this image had lost all power to hurt me. Now I had to adjust myself to the sight of her as a tall woman with a mouton fur piece, and I clenched my teeth to put down the pain I felt inside. They had been walking very slowly, just as Francesca said. He had left the house at three o'clock that afternoon, saying that he had some long-neglected law cases to attend to at the office. And when I saw them it was half-past four. Obviously he lied to me all the time without a qualm, without a single muscle of his face betraying him. He had taken his hat off the rack, slipped on his raincoat, and gone out at his usual brisk pace.

Darkness was coming on when he returned to the house. I was still lying on the sofa while the baby played with the cat and Gemma set the dining-room table. Alberto went into his study and called out to me to follow. When I looked at his face I knew that he had seen me too. He looked as if he had been through a wringer, and he had hardly any voice at all.

'We can't go on living together,' he said.

'No,' I replied.

'It's not your fault,' he said. 'You've done everything a woman could do. You've been a perfect dear and given me a great deal. But perhaps you were right to say that I was too old to get used to having a wife and child. I'm still tied to my past. And I can't go on.' He looked at me and waited for me to speak. Then, when I said nothing, he continued: 'It's not just what you think. I shan't go and live with anyone else. I need to be alone. That's the way I want to live from now on. I hate this perpetual lying to you. I have too much respect for you to tell you lies. It makes me feel oppressed and guilty. I want to be alone and at peace.'

'You're not going to live with Giovanna?' I asked.

'No,' he said, 'I swear to that.'

'Not that I care,' I added. 'What can it matter to me if

we're not together? Why don't you want to live with her,
though?'

'I don't, that's all. She has a husband and son. We met too
late. That's the way it always happens. But I'm very much
attached to her, and it disgusts me to live with another
woman.'

'It disgusts you?'

'Yes.'

'It disgusts you to live with me? I disgust you?'

'No,' he said. 'That's not it. It disgusts me to tell so many
lies.'

'"It disgusts me to live with another woman," that's what
you said, isn't it?'

'Don't plague me. Don't plague me that way, I beg of you.
I don't remember what I said. I only meant that I don't
think it's fair for me to tie you down. You're still young and
you might find happiness with another man.'

'But there's the baby. You remember that, don't you?'

'I'll come to see you often. You must stay here and I'll
take a room outside. I'll come, never fear. We'll always be
friends.'

'We shan't be friends at all. We never have been. You've
never been even a friend to me or a husband either. But I
shouldn't be happy with another man. If I were to make love
with another man I'd always see your face. I shall never be
able to get away from that. It's not so simple as you think.'

'I never said it was simple. You'll have to be very brave.
But you're honest and courageous, too. That's what attracted
me to you. Because I'm neither one nor the other. Oh, I
know myself very well.'

'And Giovanna?' I asked. 'What's she like?'

'Don't plague me,' he said. 'If you knew how difficult it
is for me to speak of her to you. It's something that's been
going on for years and years, and I don't really know what it's
about. Eleven years it's lasted and we've become very close

to one another. We've felt very unhappy and suffered together and made each other suffer. She's been unfaithful and
lied to me, and we've said all sorts of cruel things to each other
and given up the affair completely. Then we've come together again, and every time, even after so many years, it's
like something brand new. She suffered a lot when I married
you. I was glad to know that she was suffering on my account.
God knows I'd suffered often enough on hers. I thought it
would go smoothly and then I could forget her. But when we
two started living together it was terribly painful for me to be
with you instead of with her. I wanted to have a child with
you just as she had one with another man. I wanted to talk
about "my child" when she talked about hers and to have a
private life of my own which should be just as mysterious to
her as hers was to me. We've said good-bye so many times,
only to start all over again. Now I just can't live with you
any longer. I'll take a room somewhere and live by myself.
Then I'll come often to see the baby. Who knows, we may
really be better friends than we are now. Perhaps it won't be
so hard for me to talk with you about a lot of things.'

'Very well,' I said. 'As you like.'

'You're a fine girl,' he murmured. He looked exhausted,
and his voice was worn out from having talked for so long
about himself. He didn't want any supper and neither did I,
so we had a cup of tea in the study.

Then I had to put the baby to sleep by singing her the
song of *Le bon roi Dagobert*. It took her a long time to fall off.
Finally I laid her in her crib, covered her up, and stood there
looking down at her for a while. Alberto came in to look at
her, too, for a minute and then went away.

I got undressed and looked in the mirror at my naked
body, which now belonged to no man. I was free to do what
I wanted. I could go for a trip with Francesca and the baby,
for instance. I could make love with any man who happened
to catch my fancy. I could read books and see new places and

discover how other people lived. In fact, I ought to do all
of these things. I had made a mess of my life, but there was
still time to set it straight. If I made enough of an effort I
could turn into quite a different woman. After I had gone to
bed I lay for a long time staring into the darkness, and I felt
the growth of a new cold-blooded resolution inside me.

The next day I wrote to ask my mother if she would keep
the baby at Maona for a while, as she had said for some time
that she wanted to do. My father came to the city and took
Gemma and the baby away with him. The baby struggled in
Gemma's arms and called for me. I went away from the
window and stuck my fingers in my ears in order not to hear
her cries. I had to have a rest and to get away from *Le bon roi
Dagobert*. I went to see Francesca and found Augusto there.
This wasn't the first time I had come upon them together
and I began to think they might be lovers. Francesca was
painting with an expression of concentration on her face
while Augusto sat reading and smoking his pipe at the table.

'I've seen the cauliflower, do you know?' I announced.

Francesca looked at me in a puzzled way; then she caught
on and burst out laughing.

'She doesn't dress well, does she?' she said.

'I don't know,' I said. 'She had on a mouton fur piece.'

Augusto knit his brows because he didn't understand.

'Alberto and I are breaking up,' I added.

'At last!' Francesca exclaimed. She took me into the
bathroom and laid her hands on my shoulders. 'See that
you're smart now and get every penny out of him you can,'
she said. 'Always be smart, remember. That ratty little
man.'

Augusto went out with me when I left. It was a clear,
windy afternoon and heavy, white cloud scudded across the
sky. He asked me if I felt like walking and I said I did. We
walked haphazardly along the river and then up a weedy
alley to a large square overlooking the city. We could hear

distant train and factory whistles, and trams went by below us, ringing their bells and raising sparks on the overhead wire among the leaves of the trees. The wind ruffled my hair and whipped up Augusto's scarf across his distracted and indifferent face. In the middle of the square there was a bronze statue of a woman holding a sheaf of wheat, and we sat down on the stone pedestal. I asked Augusto if he was in love with Francesca and he said no, but I didn't believe it. It floated into my mind that when it was all over between them I might make love with Augusto, and for some reason this prospect left me very calm. Looking at his black moustache, his nose reddened from the cold, and his hard, lonely face, I hadn't the slightest desire to make love with him. But there was plenty of time ahead and I might change my mind.

'So you and Alberto have decided to part company,' he said.

'No,' I said. 'It's his idea, really. Perhaps it's all for the best.'

He filled his pipe with tobacco from his pouch, which he was holding between his knees, and looked down at the ground, shaking his head.

'There's just one thing I'd like to ask you,' I said. 'Do you ever see Giovanna?'

'Every now and then,' he said. 'Why?'

'I wish you'd tell her to come and see me some day. Not for the reason you may think. I don't want to make a scene or arouse her pity. I just want to speak to her, that's all. After that I think my mind would be at rest. I've thought about her so often and tried to imagine what we'd say to one another if we were to meet. It's not healthy to be completely in the dark and let one's imagination run riot. If I could really see her at last, perhaps I might be able to put the whole thing behind me.'

'I don't think Alberto would be very pleased,' he said.

'I know that,' I admitted. 'He wouldn't like it at all. He hates even to speak of her to me. He hates to think that we both exist and that one day we might even meet. He has to shuttle quite independently between us and live a double life. But I'm sick of thinking of things that it hurts him to have me think about. And I'm sick of not hurting him, too. I'm sick of being alone and in the dark, analysing my own thoughts.'

Augusto puffed at his pipe and looked into the distance. The air was unusually clear, the wind blew in warmer gusts, and the clouds hovered over the mountain-tops. Augusto's scarf blew fitfully now, and his serious, stolid face gave me a feeling of stability. We went back down the hill, and I looked back at the woman with the sheaf of wheat, raising her bronze breasts into the bright clear air. I would remember her, I said to myself, and think of this day if Augusto and I ever became lovers.

'I was in love with Giovanna myself years ago,' he said. I didn't answer right away. It was as if I had always known something of the sort. 'That was when I got the revolver,' he added.

'What revolver?'

'Alberto and I each bought one. We were all for committing suicide. We decided to shoot ourselves, each one of us in his own room, at exactly the same minute. I stared all night long at that revolver lying on my table and couldn't screw up my courage to go through with it. In the morning I went with my heart in my boots to Alberto's. But lo and behold, he was just getting ready to come and find me! We looked at each other and burst out laughing! Ever since then we've kept our revolvers loaded in our desks. I look at mine every once in a while, but I haven't any wish to shoot myself. All that was years ago. There are times when you're fed up with everything, but then the days and years sweep you along with them and you acquire some understanding. You understand that there's some meaning to even the stupidest things, and you don't take them as hard as you did before.'

I realized that he was speaking in this vein for my benefit and trying in his own way to console me. I was grateful, but there was nothing I could say.

'Yes, it was a long time ago,' he repeated. 'All night long I stared at that revolver. Giovanna was going with someone else then, an orchestra conductor, and I couldn't stand the thought of her being crazy about him. I wanted her to leave her husband and the other man, too, and come and live with me. Alberto was in love with her, too, and we wandered around the city like madmen, stopping to drink in every bar. What fools we were! Well, we didn't kill ourselves; we just went on raving together. Finally one day it dawned on me that the orchestra conductor had dropped out of the picture and Alberto was his successor. He didn't have the nerve to tell me himself and wrapped the whole thing in mystery the way he does with you now. But I was past caring. I decided it wasn't worth while losing my head over anybody, and I began to study and write a book about the Polish wars of secession. I thought Alberto wouldn't last long with her either, and instead they've gone on with it until to-day. When I saw Giovanna again we became good friends, and I stayed friends with Alberto too. We reminisce quite often about that day when we had an urge to commit suicide. We're the damnedest fools when we're young!'

When we got back to the centre of town I said good-bye to Augusto and went home. Gemma was away and I had to cook supper, so I put the meat and potatoes on the stove. I missed the baby and wished I could sing to her about *Le bon roi Dagobert*. I hummed the tune while I was setting the table. When Alberto came in I asked him when he intended to go away. He sat down at the table and propped the newspaper up in front of him without making any reply. Finally he said in a low squeaky voice:

'Are you so anxious to get rid of me?'

'No,' I said, 'take your time.'

But after supper he went into the study and began to pack his belongings in a zinc case. He dusted his books one by one as he put them in and took down the bust of Napoleon and his fleet of miniature ships. I watched him from the door. At a certain point he felt bored and sat down to read. I swept the kitchen and then went to bed.

She came on a Sunday. Augusto phoned me in the morning to tell me she would come, and in the afternoon he took Alberto to his apartment to listen to some new Negro records. I combed my hair and powdered my face and sat down to wait. All of a sudden I heard the ring of the bell at the garden gate. I pressed the button and heard the click it made when it opened. My hands were covered with a cold sweat; I clenched my teeth and swallowed hard. Then Giovanna walked in and we sat down in the drawing-room face to face.

I saw that she was embarrassed, and this simplified everything. There was a blush on her cheeks, which gradually faded away, leaving her skin pale and of a cold, flourlike consistency. 'So this is Giovanna,' I said to myself as we sized each other up. She was hatless and had on her mouton fur piece, which appeared old and worn now that I could see it from close by. She held her gloves in her hands and sat with her legs crossed in the armchair near the window. I had imagined her as a vulgar sort of woman with a great deal of make-up and a violent cut to her features and body. Of all the mental pictures I had made of her the definitive one was violent and garish. But in real life there was nothing vulgar about her. Only after several minutes did I see that she was actually beautiful. Her face was pale and cold and her full, unpainted lips were smiling silently. She had small, white teeth, blue eyes, and her long narrow head with the grey-streaked black hair pinned up on top of it was turned slightly to one side.

'Where's the baby?' she asked.

'She's not here,' I answered. 'She's with my mother in the country.'

'Too bad,' she said. 'I'd like to see her.'

'I asked you to come here,' I said. 'Perhaps you're thinking it was an odd thing to do. . . . As a matter of fact, I haven't anything in particular to say. I was curious to see you, that's all. It was a pointless sort of curiosity, when you come down to it.' She listened quietly, with her legs crossed and her worn gloves between her long fingers. 'I have no intention of hurling accusations in your face or of getting down on my knees and begging you for mercy. I don't hate you, at least not so far as I know. There's nothing to do about it, I realize that. Alberto's going away. Then you'll be able to meet more often without his telling me lies. He says he hates to lie, but I don't know whether he really means it. We don't get on well together, that's the truth. Perhaps it's not your fault. I've done all I could to make a go of it, but with no luck. It's been a mess.'

'It's warm in here,' she said, taking off her fur. She had on a green knitted dress with a red *G* embroidered over the left breast. The dress wasn't especially pretty, and she had large, heavy breasts, wide hips, and thin arms and legs. She looked around and remarked: 'The house is just the same. I used to come here sometimes when Alberto's mother was alive.'

'You came to call on the old lady?'

'Yes,' she said, laughing, 'I came to play draughts with her. She was very fond of me. But she was a terrible tyrant. It's a good thing she died, because she'd have made life miserable for you. You'd have had to play draughts all day long, and if you'd forgotten yourself and won a game she'd never have forgiven you!'

'It's been miserable enough without that,' I said.

Then she asked me if I had a picture of the baby. I showed

her one, and after she had laid it down she drew a picture out of her own handbag.

'This is my son,' she said. And I looked at a boy with bright eyes and full lips, wearing a sailor suit. 'He won't study,' she said. 'Boys are hard to handle. It's much better to have a girl. He won't do his Latin. But the teachers are too hard on them.'

I made tea and we drank it with some biscuits that she said were very good. The muscles of my face were taut and I felt very tired and ready for her to go. I wanted to ask her about the orchestra conductor and how she had met Alberto and fallen in love with him. But all I said was:

'Do you love him very much?'

'Yes,' she said. 'Very much indeed.' She put her cup down on the table and both of us stood up.

'It's been eleven years now,' she said. 'I couldn't give him up.' All of a sudden tears came into her eyes. 'No, I couldn't possibly do it. I've thought of it often enough. I've been unfaithful and lied to him and said the cruellest things. We've sworn to put an end to it, then we've begun all over again, and I may say that now I know how much I love him. I can't give him up. I'm sorry.' She pulled out a handkerchief and dabbed at her eyes. Then she blew her nose and rubbed her face, shaking her head at the same time. 'I've been unhappy; I was on poor terms with my husband from the start. I'd have left him long ago if it weren't for the boy. He's not a bad man and I suppose he loves me in his own way. But we haven't anything to say to each other and he thinks I'm silly and queer. For a long time I thought I really was as silly and queer as he said. I tried to live up to what he expected of me; I went out and gave little tea-parties and chatted with all the ladies. Then I was bored to death and gave up trying. He was terribly angry at first and made dreadful scenes, but finally he got over it and we settled down to tolerating one another. That's the way it's been with me.'

She put on her fur and gloves and tied a net scarf around her neck. 'If I'd married Alberto,' she said, 'I might have been a different woman. Stronger and braver and more energetic. And perhaps he would have been a different man. Don't think I like him the way he is now. I know his weaknesses very well, and sometimes I find him positively hateful. But if we two had married it wouldn't have been the same. We met too late. We're stupid and don't know what we really want when we're young. Life runs away with us before we know what it's all about.'

She took my hands in hers and squeezed them. She had a sad, hesitant smile on her face; perhaps she was wondering whether or not we should kiss each other good-bye. I put my face close to her cold face and had the scent of it in my nostrils for a second while we kissed.

'Too bad I didn't see the baby,' she said as we went down the stairs.

After she was gone I realized that there were other things I wanted to say to her. But I was relieved to be alone and feel the muscles of my face gradually relaxing. I lay down on the sofa with a cushion under my head. It was dark outside. I always missed the baby when evening came and wondered if my mother was tucking her in tightly so that she wouldn't toss the blankets off in her sleep. I went into the kitchen and lit the gas under a kettle of soup. Then I called the cat and threw him some scraps of cheese.

I had thought that after seeing Giovanna I should feel more peaceful, and as a matter of fact I did. An icy calm spread through me. Where before there were fantastic but silent images, now I saw a woman drinking a cup of tea and showing me a picture of her son. I felt neither hate nor pity. I felt nothing at all. Inside there was a great black hole that made me even lonelier than before. Now I realized that those silent images of Giovanna had somehow peopled my solitude and kept me company. I was alone now, and when my hand groped for the picture I had made of her it found only an empty black hole and withdrew with a withering chill upon it. The real Giovanna who had sat in the armchair near the window did not hate me, and I did not hate her; indeed, there was no relationship of any kind between us.

I wondered when Alberto was going away and wished it would be soon. But he couldn't seem to make up his mind. I watched the bookshelves gradually empty themselves as every day he packed a few more books away in the zinc case. When they were altogether empty, I thought to myself, he would go away. We hardly talked to each other at all. I made lunch and supper and ironed his shirts because Gemma was away. He polished his own shoes and sometimes he helped me clear the table. Every morning I made his bed while he stood by the window waiting for me to finish.

I didn't tell him about Giovanna's visit, nor did I know whether or not she had told him. A few days later I went to Maona to get the baby. I meant to tell my mother that Alberto and I were separating, but when I saw her I didn't say anything. She was slicing ham in the kitchen when I arrived, and the baby had a cold. I said she must have tossed off the blankets in her sleep, and at this both my mother and father took offence. I went back in the bus with the baby in my arms and Gemma weeping like a fountain beside me because she was leaving her family. While we were rolling among the hills and fields that bordered the highway I held the baby tight and tried to imagine the time when we would be alone together. My mother had pinned her hair up in two braids around her head, and her thin, bare face had a new alert but melancholy expression. I had a feeling that she knew what had happened. She sat on my knees, crumbling a biscuit in her fingers and putting an occasional piece in her mouth. She didn't talk yet, but she seemed to understand everything. When we reached home we met Alberto coming out of the gate. He took the baby in his arms and kissed her, but she only started to cry. He set her down on the ground, shrugged his shoulders, and went on his way.

I telephoned Francesca, and when she came to see me I asked her if she felt like taking that long-delayed trip to San Remo with the baby and me. I told her that probably Alberto would leave in the next few days and I didn't want to be around and see him go. She was very pleased and said we'd go to the Hotel Bellevue, where they served hot ice-cream every Saturday night. I asked her what that was and she said it was vanilla ice-cream with a hot chocolate sauce over it. She looked up the trains and made all the arrangements in no time at all.

When Alberto came home he found me packing my bags. This time it was my turn to be going somewhere without him and he looked on in glum silence. I told him that Gemma would stay to look after him and asked him for some money, which he gave me. We left early the next morning while he was still asleep.

San Remo was very windy. At first we were all in one room, but Francesca couldn't stand the baby's crying and took another room for herself. For some days she hung about us and said that San Remo was a resort for doddering old gentlemen and she was bored to death with it.

Then she made friends with some people at the hotel and went out boating and dancing with them. She had any number of evening dresses, each one more beautiful than the next. I stayed with the baby until she fell asleep, and then I went downstairs with my knitting, but I was always afraid that the baby might wake up and cry, so I went to bed very early. When Francesca came up she knocked at my door and I went into her room and heard who had danced with her and what they had to say.

After we had been there a fortnight Augusto came to join us. He was ill-humoured and jealous, and Francesca treated him very shabbily. He sat smoking in the hotel lobby and wrote a chapter of his new book on the origins of Christianity. I asked him if Alberto were at the house and he said that he was still slowly packing his books in the zinc case. I wanted to talk to him about Giovanna, but he cut me short because he was in too gloomy a mood to listen. Sometimes he walked silently up and down the pavement with the baby and me, looking around for Francesca's plaid coat. Francesca didn't want him about. She had made friends with a countess, and every night she got drunk with her and they went to the casino. She was bored with all her evening dresses and made herself a new one out of a long black skirt and some silk scarves sewed together. She painted a picture of the countess stretched out on a tiger skin and she was always telling me that the countess's children weren't little pests like mine.

The baby had begun to talk. Every day she said something new and I thought she was very clever. When she had eaten her biscuit she stretched out both hands and said: 'More!' with a wily, melancholy smile. Every morning she stood up in her bed and said: 'Baby sleep no more!' and I would take her and the camel into my bed and make the camel walk up and down on the bedcover. Then Francesca would come in wearing a wrapper, with cold cream on her face and her hair in curlers, smoke a cigarette, and tell me between yawns about the evening she had spent with the countess.

I told her she ought to be a little nicer to Augusto. She was heartless, I told her, to lead him a life like this. Every now and then they went for a walk together, and perhaps they found a place to make love somewhere because he always seemed slightly more cheerful when they returned. But then the countess and her friends whistled under Francesca's window and she powdered her face in a hurry, threw on her plaid coat, and ran to join them. I never knew whether she had taken a liking to one of the men in the party or not. She said no. She said that they were amusing, while Augusto

was solemn and jealous and his origins of Christianity bored
her to death.

The baby was taken ill on November seventeenth. She
was upset all day long and would not eat. It was Saturday
and they served the famous hot ice-cream, but she cried and
spat it all over the place, until I lost patience and struck her
across the hands. She cried and cried, and I didn't know what
to do. She didn't want to hear about *Le bon roi Dagobert* or
have her camel beside her or anything. She cried steadily until
ten o'clock in the evening, and then she fell asleep. I lowered
her gently into the bed and sat down beside her. She slept for
half an hour or so, but very lightly, shifting about and twitching at intervals. Francesca dropped in to see me on her way
to a dance at the casino. She had combed her hair back from
her forehead in a strange new way and painted her lips a
colour that was almost yellow. She had on what she called her
Hindu dress, the one made of silk scarves sewed together, and
a wide silver lamé sash around her waist. The effect was
really stunning. She looked down at the baby and said she
must have worms to twitch that way in her sleep. She walked
around the room, and I hated her for making so much noise.
Then the countess whistled under the window and off she
went.

While she was running down the hall the baby woke up
screaming and I picked her up in my arms. She seemed burning hot, and so I took her temperature. The thermometer
read 102. I paced up and down the room with her, wondering
what could be the matter. She was breathing hard and twisting her lips. It couldn't be just an ordinary fever. She had
been feverish a number of times, but never before had she
cried so desperately. I tried asking her what hurt, but she only
cried louder and pushed away my hands. I was terrified.
Finally I laid her down on the bed and went to call Augusto.
He was lying fully dressed on his bed with the light on, and

there was a distressed look in his half-closed eyes because Francesca had gone to the dance without him. I told him that the baby was very sick and asked him to go and get a doctor. He sat up and smoothed his hair without really understanding what I had said. Then he pulled himself together and put on his overcoat. I went back to my room, picked up the baby, and paced up and down, holding her wrapped in a blanket. She had a red face and excessively bright eyes. Every now and then she fell asleep, only to wake up again with a start. I thought of how men and women spend their time tormenting one another and how stupid it all seems when you are face to face with something like a baby's fever. I remembered how once upon a time I had tormented myself waiting tremblingly for Alberto and wondered how I could have attached importance to anything so idiotic. I was badly frightened, but beneath my fright there was a feeling that the baby was going to get well and Francesca would tease me for being such an alarmist. So many times before I had been scared to death over nothing at all.

Then Augusto came back with the doctor, a red-haired young man with a freckled face. I hurriedly and nervously undressed the baby on the bed. She was crying more feebly now as the doctor held her thin little body in his hands and Augusto looked on in silence. The doctor said that he couldn't diagnose her trouble, but he saw no reason for concern. He prescribed a mild sedative and Augusto went to have it made up at a pharmacy. Then the doctor went away, saying he would come back in the morning. Augusto stayed with me and I felt much calmer. The baby went to sleep and I looked at her thin, red face and perspiration-drenched hair. I asked Augusto not to go away because I was still frightened to be alone.

At three o'clock in the morning the baby screamed. She grew purple in the face and threw up the small portion of ice-cream I had forced down her the evening before. She waved

her arms and legs and pushed me away. The chamber-
maid and a woman who had the room next to mine came in
and suggested I give her an enema prepared with camomile.
While I was preparing it Francesca appeared at the door,
looking very drunk. Hating her with all my might, I shouted:
'Go away!'

She went into her room and came back a few minutes later,
after she had apparently bathed her face in cold water. She
asked the maid to get her a cup of strong coffee. I hated her
so much that I couldn't look her in the face. My throat was
dry and constricted with terror. The baby was not crying
any more; she lay there under the blanket with all the colour
gone out of her cheeks, breathing jerkily.

'You nincompoops!' said Francesca. 'Can't you see she's
in a very bad way? You've got to get a doctor.'

The maid told her that one had already come, but
Francesca said none of the San Remo doctors was any good
except the countess's doctor. She spoke in a loud voice and a
decisive manner, as if to show that she was no longer drunk.
She went out to look for the countess's doctor, and Augusto
went with her, leaving me alone with the woman who had
suggested the enema. Her face was heavy and wrinkled, with
powder caked in the furrows; she wore a violet kimono and
spoke with a strong German accent. For some reason her
presence was very reassuring; I had complete confidence in
her heavy, wrinkled face. She told me that the baby must
have an upset stomach and such a disturbance often takes on
terrifying forms. Her son had had an attack of the same kind
when he was a baby. And now he was a grown man—she
raised her hand to show me how tall he was—who had taken
a degree in engineering and got himself engaged to be
married.

It was growing light outside. The sun rose out of a greenish
haze and shone upon the sea. On the terrace in front of the
hotel a waiter in a white jacket was setting wicker chairs and

tables in order among the palms, and another man in a striped outfit was dipping a mop into a bucket of water. Now the sun was red and glaring. I hated the sea and the wicker furniture and the palm trees. Why had I come to San Remo anyhow? What was I doing in this room with the woman in a violet kimono? I hated Francesca and thought to myself that she and Augusto must have stopped at the countess's for drinks and have had one too many.

They did come back, though, with the countess's doctor, a tall, bald man with a thin, ivory face and a pendulous lower lip, disclosing teeth that were long and yellow like those of a horse. He said that neither the sedative nor the enema was any use. Everything that had been done so far was wrong. He wrote out another prescription, and while Augusto went back to the pharmacy he questioned me about the baby's health in recent months and how she had been taken ill. While I was telling him he held the camel in his hand and made it walk up and down the rug. Somehow his gesture gave me hope. I asked him if it was something serious and he said he didn't think so but he couldn't yet say for sure. He could advance various hypotheses, but none of them was definitive. He sent away the woman in the kimono because he said there should be as few people as possible in a sickroom in order to conserve the supply of oxygen. Francesca brought me a cup of coffee. It was a bright, sunny day, and the usual old gentlemen were sitting on the terrace, holding their canes between their knees and reading their newspapers.

At nine o'clock, just as the bald doctor was cleaning a syringe in order to make an injection, the freckled-faced doctor of the previous evening came back. He seemed a little offended, but Francesca took him out in the hall and talked to him in private. Then the two doctors held a consultation together. The baby was quiet now and breathing evenly. She seemed very tired, with white lips and dark circles around her eyes. She stood up on the bed and said:

'Sleep no more!'

These were the first words she had spoken since she had fallen ill, and I was so happy that I burst into tears. Francesca held me in her arms.

'I thought she was going to die,' I murmured. Francesca patted my shoulders without speaking. 'I thought she was going to die for certain. I thought so all night long. I was scared to death.' I wanted to make up to Francesca somehow for the hate I had felt for her at three o'clock in the morning. 'You looked very handsome in your Hindu dress. And the way you had your hair fixed was very becoming.'

'Don't you think we ought to send a wire to Alberto?' she said. 'She's the poor devil's daughter, after all.'

'Yes,' I said. 'But isn't she better?'

'Perhaps so,' she said. 'But I'd send him a wire just the same.'

At eleven o'clock the baby began to scream again, shaking and twitching all over, with a fever of 103. In the afternoon she fell asleep but only for a few minutes. Augusto went to send the wire. I began to wish Alberto would arrive immediately. I paced up and down the room, holding the baby wrapped in a blanket. Francesca stepped out in the hall every now and then for a cigarette. The doctor went out to dinner and came back. I could read no hope in his gloomy, disdainful face with the pendulous lower lip. Everyone looked as if there were no hope, and I wanted to tell them that I knew she was better. She looked better to me, and for a moment, when she was in Francesca's arms, she began to play with her necklace.

'Le bon roi Dagobert
Chassait dans la plaine de l'Enfer!'

Men and women strolled along the pavement or sat comfortably in the wicker chairs among the palm trees. They smoked cigarettes, flicked the ashes away, tucked plaid blankets around their legs, and showed each other cartoons in the papers. A boy came by selling fresh oranges, and they pressed them in their fingers and counted the change in the palms of their hands.

> ' Le bon roi Dagobert
> A mis sa culotte à l'envers!'

I remembered with horror how I had struck the baby across the hands when she would not eat her supper and how she had thrown down her spoon and started to cry disconsolately. I looked into her big brown eyes and thought that she knew all there was to know about me. Her eyes were weary and dull, and their lack of expression was dreadful on a baby's face. She had a faraway, bitter look, unreproaching but at the same time pitiless, as if she had nothing more to ask. I stopped rocking her in my arms and laid her down on the bed under a shawl. She sobbed convulsively and pushed away my hands.

Suddenly Francesca began to cry and went out of the room. I looked at the doctor and he looked at me. His damp, red, pendulous lower lip gave him the appearance of an animal drinking. The freckled doctor came back with another, smaller doctor who seemed to be someone very important. I asked them if I should undress the baby and they said no. The little doctor felt her neck and forehead and tapped her knees with an ivory stick. Then they went away. I was left alone with the bald doctor, and all of a sudden his pendulous lower lip reminded me of something indecent, like the sexual parts of a dog. Then he told me it might be meningitis. At ten o'clock in the evening the baby died.

Francesca took me into her room and I lay down on her bed and drank a cup of coffee. The woman in the violet kimono and the manager of the hotel and the freckled-faced doctor all came to see me. The woman told me I'd have other children. She said that when children die young it isn't so bad. It's worse when they're older. She had lost a son who was a lieutenant in the Navy, and she raised her hand to show me how tall he was. But the hotel manager said it was harder to lose children when they were small. Finally Francesca sent them all away and told me to go to sleep.

I shut my eyes, but there was one sight I couldn't get away from. It was the expression in the baby's face when I was rocking her in my arms. Her eyes were bitter and indifferent, indifferent even to *Le bon roi Dagobert*. I could see all her clothes and toys: the camel, the ball, the squeaking rubber cat, the leggings, the galoshes, and the apron with Snow White and the Seven Dwarfs on it. I remembered the things she ate and the words she knew how to say. Then I fell asleep and dreamed I was walking along a road and bumped up against a stone wall, which made me wake up screaming.

I called Francesca, but she wasn't in the room. There was only Augusto, standing by the window with his head against the glass. He said Francesca had gone in to the baby and asked me if there was anything I wanted. I asked him to sit down beside me, and he sat there, holding my hand and stroking my hair. Then I began to cry. I cried all night long, with my face buried in the pillow. I hung on to his hand and said things that made no sense. As long as I cried or talked I could forget about the camel and the ball. Alberto arrived at five o'clock in the morning. He dropped his bag and ran sobbing to kneel down beside me, and his head of curly grey hair on my shoulder seemed to be the only thing in the world I needed.

I told Alberto that I never wanted to see the camel or the ball again, and Francesca and he made a bundle of all the baby's things and gave them away. Francesca left San Remo several days before us and removed from the house the baby's carriage, crib, and all the rest of her belongings. At the same

time she told Gemma to go and pay a visit to her family at
Maona. Gemma left in tears, taking the cat with her. I
couldn't bear to see her because I should have been reminded
of the stye in her eye when she bent over me the day the baby
was born. Alberto wrote to my mother and father that I didn't
want to see them but preferred to be alone with him for a
while. I didn't want anyone else, and they must be patient and
let me fill my own needs as I thought best. Everyone reacts
to sorrow in his own particular way, he told them, and throws
up the best defences he can. And in such cases the family and
friends must hold their peace and stand by quietly until it is
over.

We went back to the city, and for a while I didn't leave
the house because I didn't want to see any children. At first
a woman came to do the cleaning, but it was so hard for me to
talk to her that finally I told her not to come and did the work
myself. Still I didn't have very much to do. I stayed in bed
late in the morning, watching my arms lie empty and free on
the bedcover. Then I slowly got dressed and let the empty hours
of the day drag by. I tried not to think of the song about *Le
bon roi Dagobert*, but it rang continually in my ears. And I
still saw in front of me the doctor's mouth, like that of an
animal drinking, the long halls and red-carpeted stairways of
the Hotel Bellevue and the wicker chairs and palm trees on
the terrace below.

Alberto stayed at home a great deal. He was extremely
kind, and I was amazed by his efforts to help me. We never
mentioned the baby, and I noticed that he had taken away
the oatmeal and the rest of her food that Francesca had
forgotten. He read Rilke's poems out loud and also some of
the notes he had written on the margins of various books.
He said that some day or other he wanted to put all these notes
together in a volume which he would call *Variations on a
Minor Scale*. I think he was slightly envious of Augusto for
the books he had published. Anyhow, he said I was to help put

the notes in order, and sometimes he had me work over them on the typewriter until late at night. I didn't type fast enough to keep up with his dictation, but he never lost his temper. He even told me that I should make comments on anything that didn't seem clear to me.

One day I asked him if he was going away and he said no. Sooner or later, he said, he'd empty the zinc case where he'd begun to pack his books. Meanwhile it sat there in his study, half filled with his things. When he wanted one particular book he had quite a time digging it out, but still he didn't get around to putting everything back on the shelves. We spent most of the time in the study, and he never said a word about wanting to go out. At first we didn't talk about the baby, but later we did, and he said perhaps it was good for me to unburden myself to him. He said that we'd have another child and that even if now this prospect gave me no pleasure, I would love the new one just as well, and all my peace of mind would come back to me when I saw it lying at my side. We made love together and gradually I began to imagine the time when I would have another baby. I thought of how I would nurse it and rock it, and of all my thoughts this was the only one from which I got any satisfaction.

Then I began to fall in love again with Alberto, and the realization of it frightened me. I trembled now at the idea of his going away, and the sight of the zinc case became painful. When I typed to his dictation I was afraid of going too slowly, and when he looked at me I imagined that he didn't like my face. I reflected how easy everything was for other women—Francesca and Giovanna, for instance, who never seemed to have known even the shadow of my great fear. How easy life is, I thought, for women who are not afraid of a man. I stared for a long time at my face in the mirror. It had never been very pretty, and now it seemed to me that every trace of youth and freshness was gone.

Alberto and I were always at home, and I understood now

how a man and woman live together. He never went out, and I saw him from one end of the day to the other. I saw him get up in the morning and drink the cup of coffee I had made for him; I saw him bend over and dig into the zinc case and make notes on the margins of his books. We made love on his couch in the study and lay awake in the darkness while I felt him breathing calmly beside me. Before going to sleep he always told me to wake him up if I felt sad. I didn't dare actually wake him, but the thought that I could if I wanted to was a great consolation. He was so very kind that now I knew what a man's tenderness could be. It was my own fault, I realized, if even now I wasn't altogether happy with him. I was always worried about my face and body, and when we made love I was afraid he might be bored. Every time I had something to say to him I thought it over to make sure it wasn't boring. When he read me the notes he wanted to make into a book occasional comments came into my mind. But when one day I finally said something he seemed displeased and explained to me at length why I was wrong. I could have bitten off my tongue for having spoken. I remembered the time before we were married when we sat endlessly in cafés and I babbled on without stopping. Then it was easy enough for me to talk. I said whatever came into my head and moved before him with all the confidence of youth. Now that I had had the baby and the baby was dead I couldn't bear the idea of his leaving me.

'Why *don't* you go away?' I said. 'I know it's just that you're sorry for me. Why don't you go?'

'I don't like the idea of your being here alone,' he replied.

'I never expected you to be so kind,' I went on. 'I didn't dream you'd try to help me as much as you've done. I didn't think you cared much for the baby or for me either. I thought you cared only for Giovanna.'

He chuckled quietly, as if to himself. 'Sometimes I think I don't care for anyone,' he said.

'Not even for Giovanna?'

'No, not even for Giovanna,' he said. 'She and her husband have gone to their country house near the lakes, and I don't know when she'll be back. When I don't see her I hardly ever think of her at all. Queer, isn't it?'

We were silent for a few minutes. He lay at my side breathing quietly, toying with my hand on the bedcover. He opened my fingers and closed them suddenly; he tickled my palm, then put my hand down and drew away.

'It's difficult to know what we have inside of us. We're here to-day and gone to-morrow. I've never understood myself properly. I was very fond of my mother, for instance, and terribly sad to see her go. Then one morning I walked out of the house with a cigarette in my mouth, and just as I was striking a match to light it I had a sudden feeling of relief. I was almost glad that she was dead, that I would never have to play draughts with her again or hear her irritated tone of voice when I put too much sugar in her coffee. That's how it is that I don't really know how much I care for Giovanna. I haven't seen her for several months now, and I can't say I've thought very much about her. I'm lazy, when you come down to it, and I don't want to suffer.'

'And when she comes back,' I said, 'do you think you'll want to go away?'

'I don't know,' he answered. 'I might, at that.'

As I lay awake I remembered that he had told me to call him whenever I felt too sad. But I didn't have the nerve to do it, and besides I was beginning to realize that there was no use counting on him for anything. It was absurd to expect anything from a man like Alberto. Even Giovanna couldn't really count on him. I looked at his sleeping face, with the immobile lips that gave no answer. Would he stay or go? Did he really want to have another child? I lay there with my eyes wide open and said to myself: 'I'll never know what he really wants. I'll never know.'

It was then that I remembered the revolver. I began to think about it in somewhat the same way as I had thought of nursing another baby. The idea of it calmed me and I thought of it while I was making the bed or peeling potatoes or ironing Alberto's shirts or going up and down the stairs. If I were to have another baby I'd be in constant fear that it might take ill and die. I was tired of being afraid, and now that I understood him there didn't seem to be much point to bearing a child for Alberto.

Francesca came occasionally to see me, and she told me that she had a new lover. He was a man she had met with the countess at San Remo, and she had given up painting in order to spend all of her time with him. She said she had a weakness for him, but nothing too serious, and that he was somewhat of a gangster, so that I shouldn't be surprised if I read in the paper one day that he had strangled her in her sleep. He was strictly no good, she said, and every time he left her she went to make sure he hadn't broken into her jewellery. But he was a handsome devil, and she liked to be seen with him, because women all turned their heads to stare, and for quite some time he had been a fancy man to the countess. She said that the countess was an old bitch and a dreadful miser because she wouldn't buy the picture she had painted of her. When the countess had come back from San Remo they had had a terrible row over Francesca's new lover. Francesca didn't want to hear any more of Augusto, and Augusto didn't want to hear of her either. But Augusto came to see us very seldom because he was working hard to finish his book on the origins of Christianity.

Alberto read his notes to him and tried to interest him in his writing, but Augusto hardly paid any attention. He seemed to prefer being with me and often he hung about watching me iron shirts. I thought of the windy day when we had gone for a walk together and I had imagined making love with him. When I looked at his face I felt that he was a little like

me, with his eyes continually staring into a well of darkness
within him. For this reason I thought that we might be
happy as lovers and that he might understand and help me. But
then I told myself that it was too late, too late to start something new like falling in love or having another baby. It was
too hard work, and I was tired. Looking at Augusto, I remembered the night at San Remo when the baby was taken
ill and the night after, when I had lain clutching his hand.
There are other things in life, I told myself, than making
love or having children. There are a thousand things to do,
and one of them is writing a book on the origins of Christianity. My own life seemed to me meagre and limited, but
it was too late to change it, and back of all my thoughts now
there was always the image of the revolver.

Alberto had begun to go out again. He said that he was
going to the office, but I was sure that Giovanna must be
back. He said that she wasn't, but I didn't believe him. Then
one day Giovanna came to see me. It was in the morning, and
Alberto had gone out, leaving me to type his notes.

This time Giovanna was dressed in grey with a round,
straw hat and a sort of cape over her shoulders. Her hat and
dress were new, but she was wearing the same worn gloves as
she had worn before. She sat down and started immediately to
speak of the baby. She said that she had written me a letter
and then torn it up because it seemed silly to send it. I had
been very much in her thoughts, she said, but she hesitated a
long time before coming to see me, until finally she had put
on her hat and come. I looked at her hat, and it didn't seem
to me like a hat that had been put on in a hurry. It was a stiff
little hat, and I wondered if it didn't press against her forehead. She spoke quietly and simply, as if she were trying not
to give me pain. But I didn't want to talk to her about the
baby.

'It's very odd,' she said, 'but I dreamed about your baby
for two or three nights in succession just before she died. I

dreamed that we were in this drawing-room, and Alberto's mother was here, too, lying on the couch, wrapped in a blanket. She said that she felt cold and I threw my fur over her and she thanked me for it. The baby was sitting on a little stool, and she was afraid the baby might get a chill and asked me to shut the window. I had bought the baby a doll and I wanted to take it out of the package, but I couldn't seem to untie the string.'

'The baby didn't play with dolls,' I said. 'She played with a ball and a camel.'

'I thought the dream was a strange one,' she went on. 'I woke up in a state of anxiety, which I couldn't explain. Then a few days later I got a letter from Alberto about the baby.'

I looked at her hard and tried to make out whether she had really had any such dream. I had a strong suspicion that she was making the whole thing up.

'He wrote only a very few words,' she said. 'We had guests that day and I had to talk to them and entertain them. And all the time I was in distress. Strange to say, I wasn't thinking of Alberto as much as I was of you.'

She sat in an armchair with her slender legs crossed, her hands folded underneath her cape, and her hat perched stiffly on her head.

'That hat must hurt you,' I said.

'Yes, it does,' she answered, pulling it off and revealing a red mark on her forehead.

I looked at her hard. She had a kind and peaceful expression on her face, and her body was peaceful and cool in her new spring dress. I imagined her picking it out of a fashion journal and ordering a dressmaker to make it. I thought of the succession of peaceful days that made up her existence and of her body that knew neither uncertainty nor fear.

'Do you hate me?' she asked.

'No,' I said. 'I don't exactly hate you. But I don't want to talk to you. I don't see any point to our being in the same room. I think it's stupid and ridiculous. Because we'll never speak of really important things or be honest with one another. I don't really believe you had that dream, you know. I believe you made it up on your way here.'

'No,' she said, and began to laugh. 'I can't make things up. Hasn't Alberto told you that I have no imagination?'

'No. We don't talk much about you. Once when we did talk about you he said that he didn't think of you often when you were away. That should have made me feel better, but it only made me feel worse. It means that he doesn't love anyone, not even you. Nothing is sacred to him. Once upon a time I was jealous and hated you, but now all that's gone. Don't think for a minute that he's unhappy without you. He refuses to be unhappy. He just lights a cigarette and walks away.'

'I know,' she said. 'You can't tell me anything about him that I don't know. You forget how long I've known him. Time has gone by and now we're no longer young. We've grown old together, he in his house and I in mine, but together just the same. We've said good-bye over and over, but we've always come together again. He didn't make the first move, that's true. I did. But he was always very glad. We get on well together. You can't understand him because you started off on the wrong foot.'

'Please go away,' I said. 'If you stay any longer I shall begin to hate you.'

'Hate me, if you like,' she said. 'You're quite within your rights. Perhaps I hate you too. But I'm sorry your baby died. I have a child myself and I feel sorry for any woman who loses one. After I had read Alberto's letter I couldn't think of anything else all day. I was stunned.'

'I don't want Alberto to write you,' I said. 'I don't want you to meet and take walks and trips together and talk about

the baby and me. After all, he's my husband. Perhaps I
shouldn't have married him in the first place, but I did, and
we had a child and lost her. This can't be wiped out just
because you two enjoy making love together.'

'Perhaps what's passed between Alberto and me can't be
wiped out either,' she murmured as if to herself. She put on
her hat, frowning, and slowly pulled on her gloves, looking
at every finger.

'I don't know what there's been between you two,' I
said. 'Important things, no doubt, but not as important as
the birth and death of a baby. Little trips you've had, haven't
you ? And little walks together. But go away now, will you ?
I'm tired of seeing you there in front of me. I'm tired of your
dress and hat. I'm saying things that don't make sense. If
you stay here any longer I may want to kill you.'

'No, you won't,' she said with a shrill, youthful laugh.
'You wouldn't do a thing like that. You look like too much
of a simple country girl. And I'm not the least bit afraid of
you.'

'So much the better,' I said, 'but go away.'

'Very well, I'm going,' she said. 'But I shall remember
this day. It's a landmark, somehow. I don't know exactly
why. But I have a feeling that we've said a lot of honest and
important things to each other. I'll come to see you again, if
you don't mind.'

'I'd rather not, thank you just the same,' I said.

'Well, you say what you mean, anyhow, don't you ?' she
said. 'Don't hate me too much.' And she went away.

I went back to my typing, but I couldn't keep my mind
on it and made any number of mistakes. I went over to the
mirror to see if I really looked like a simple country girl. By
the time lunch was ready Alberto had come home. I asked
him if I looked like a simple country girl, and he looked at
me hard for a minute before he said no. Then he added that
he didn't know what a simple country girl would look like

anyhow. He was nervous and distracted and immediately after lunch he went out again.

I wanted to phone Francesca or go and see her, but I remembered that she was probably with her new lover. Alberto went back to going out every day and sometimes in the evening as well. Now that I was sleeping in the study he no longer locked the door, so very often when I was alone in the evening I opened the desk drawer and looked at the revolver. To look at it like that calmed me down, and afterwards I shut the drawer very slowly and went to bed. I lay awake in the darkness, trying not to remember the time when the baby's feeble and plaintive cry used to break the silence of the night. My thoughts carried me far away to the time when I was a child in Maona. I remembered a certain black cream that my mother used to put on my hands to cure me of chilblains, and I could see the face of an old school teacher with glasses who used to take us on picnics, and that of a monk who came every Sunday to ask charity of my mother and carried with him a grey sack full of dry crusts of bread. I thought of how I used to read *From Slavegirl to Queen* and how I had hidden in the coal cellar and wept one day when my mother had made me a pale blue dress to wear to a school party and I had thought it was very pretty and then discovered it wasn't pretty at all. I realized that I was saying good-bye to all these things, as if I were about to take leave of them for ever, and, closing my eyes, I could smell the black cream on my hands and the odour of the baked pears that my mother used to feed us in cold weather.

When Alberto came home on nights like these we would make love together. But he no longer spoke of our having any more children. He was bored with dictating notes for his book and he glanced constantly at his watch all the time that he was in the house. Sometimes it occurred to me that soon he would be too old and tired to go out and then he would sit in an armchair and dictate to me and ask me to take his things out of the zinc case, to put the books back on the shelves and the miniature ships in their accustomed place. But Alberto was just the same as ever, older and yet incorrigibly young. He walked at a brisk pace and stuck his thin head forward as if to drink in the air of the street, with his open raincoat flapping across his slight body and a lighted cigarette between his lips. Between the eyes I shot him.

He had asked me to put some tea in a thermos bottle to take with him on his trip. He had always said that I was good at making tea. I wasn't especially good at ironing or cooking, but my tea was the best he had ever tasted. He was slightly annoyed when it came to packing his bag because his shirts weren't very well ironed, particularly between the sleeves and the collar. He packed his bag alone, saying he didn't want me to help him. He put in on top several books from the zinc case. I suggested the poems of Rilke, but he turned them down.

'I know them by heart,' he said.

I put some books in my bag too. When he saw me packing he was glad and said it would do me good to go to Maona and have my mother bring me my coffee in bed in the morning. I asked him what he was going to do about the zinc case.

'The zinc case?' he said, and started to laugh. 'I'm not going away for good, you know. Did you think I was? Is that why you have such a solemn face?'

I went to look in the mirror and said:

'A very ordinary sort of face. The face of a simple country girl.'

'Yes, a simple country girl,' he said, and stroked my hair. Then he asked me to make him the tea, which he liked strong and very sweet.

'Tell me the truth, Alberto,' I said.

'What truth?' he echoed.

'You're going away together.'

'Who are going away together?' And then he added jokingly:

'*She* seeketh Truth, which is so dear
As knoweth he who life for her refuses.'

When I came back to the study he had completed the sketch. He showed it to me and laughed. It was a long, long train with a big cloud of black smoke swirling over it. He wet the tip of the pencil with his tongue in order to make the smoke thicker. I put the thermos bottle down on the desk. He was laughing and turned around to see if I was laughing too.

I shot him between the eyes.

My feet were wet and cold and my blistered heel hurt me at every step. The streets were quite empty and they glistened in the gentle rain. I wanted to go to Francesca's, but I thought probably she was with her lover. And so I went home. There was a dead silence, which I tried my very best not to hear. When I reached the kitchen I knew what I was going to do. It was very easy and I was not afraid. I knew now that I would never have to talk to the man with the olive complexion sitting behind the desk in the police station, and this genuinely relieved me. I would never talk to anyone again. Not to Francesca or Giovanna or Augusto or my mother. To no one. I sat down at the marble-top table, where I could not escape listening to the silence. A cold, rank smell came up out of the sink, and the alarm clock ticked on the shelf. I took pen and ink and began to write in the notebook where I kept an account of household expenses. All of a sudden I asked myself for whose benefit I was writing. Not for Giovanna or Francesca, not even for my mother. For whom, then? It was too difficult to decide, and I felt that the time of conventional and clear-cut answers had come for ever to a stop within me.